I, QUANTRILL

Max McCoy

A SIGNET BOOK

SIGNET
Published by New American Library, a division of
Penguin Group (USA) Inc., 375 Hudson Street,
New York, New York 10014, USA
Penguin Group (Canada), 90 Eglinton Avenue East, Suite 700, Toronto,
Ontario M4P 2Y3, Canada (a division of Pearson Penguin Canada Inc.)
Penguin Books Ltd., 80 Strand, London WC2R 0RL, England
Penguin Ireland, 25 St. Stephen's Green, Dublin 2,
Ireland (a division of Penguin Books Ltd.)
Penguin Group (Australia), 250 Camberwell Road, Camberwell, Victoria 3124,
Australia (a division of Pearson Australia Group Pty. Ltd.)
Penguin Books India Pvt. Ltd., 11 Community Centre, Panchsheel Park,
New Delhi - 110 017, India
Penguin Group (NZ), 67 Apollo Drive, Rosedale, North Shore 0632,
New Zealand (a division of Pearson New Zealand Ltd.)
Penguin Books (South Africa) (Pty.) Ltd., 24 Sturdee Avenue,
Rosebank, Johannesburg 2196, South Africa

Penguin Books Ltd., Registered Offices:
80 Strand, London WC2R 0RL, England

First published by Signet, an imprint of New American Library,
a division of Penguin Group (USA) Inc.

First Printing, May 2008
10 9 8 7 6 5 4 3 2 1

Copyright © Max McCoy, 2008
All rights reserved

 REGISTERED TRADEMARK—MARCA REGISTRADA

Printed in the United States of America

PUBLISHER'S NOTE
This is a work of fiction. Names, characters, places, and incidents either are the product
of the author's imagination or are used fictitiously, and any resemblance to actual persons, living or dead, business establishments, events, or locales is entirely coincidental.
    The publisher does not have any control over and does not assume any responsibil-
ity for author or third-party Web sites or their content.

For the bastard Johnny Boggs

Prelude

Here also flourished in ancient times those bands of gallant outlaws, whose deeds have been rendered so popular in English song.

—*Walter Scott*, Ivanhoe *(1819)*

Then comes Sir Walter Scott with his enchantments, and by his single might checks this wave of progress, and even turns it back; sets the world in love with dreams and phantoms; with decayed and swinish forms of religion; with decayed and degraded systems of government; with the sillinesses and emptinesses, sham grandeurs, sham gauds, and sham chivalries of a brainless and worthless long-vanished society. He did measureless harm; more real and lasting harm, perhaps, than any other individual that ever wrote.

—*Mark Twain*, Life on the Mississippi *(1883)*

Lawrence

Y ou'll want to know about Lawrence, of course. Everybody does. If they don't ask outright, they will make some oblique reference in hopes of sparking a conversation or perhaps an argument. So let's dispatch your curiosity in short order, while my mind is still sharp.

Allow me to set the scene at the height of the action.

It's seven o'clock on the morning of Friday, August 21, 1863.

We've been in town for nearly two hours. Pickets are stationed on the big hill south of town called Mount Oread and are keeping a lookout for Yankee columns. The telegraph hasn't crossed the Kaw River yet to join Lawrence with the rest of the world, but a fast rider could summon help on the double-quick. There isn't a breath of air stirring—it's going to be a scorcher by noon—and in the east a full moon rides high in the pale blue sky. Crows wheel overhead, attracted by the smell and the scale of the slaughter.

Four hundred and fifty riders have fanned out and are hunting down every male old enough to hold a rifle. I have compiled death lists of those who most deserve to die. Their homes are to be burned as well. There are also plenty of targets of opportunity—any structure that displays the flag of the United States is to be razed and its male occupants killed. The town has broad streets that make it easy for the raiders to race from one location to the next. The air is thick with smoke and filled with the cracking of revolvers, the thunder of hooves, and a chorus of rebel yells.

It is the largest such force ever assembled in the West—guerrillas, partisans, regular army recruits, freebooters, bushwhackers, ruffians, drunks, a parson or two, even Missouri farmers we picked up on the way—and all of them are expert shots and superb horsemen.

They fire their revolvers offhand and are as smooth in the saddle as if sitting down to Sunday dinner, but their eyes blaze with murderous intent. They drag men from their homes, ignoring the pleas of wives and daughters, and dispatch them with pistol shots with no more hesitation than one would in shooting a rabid dog.

And I'm in charge of this visitation of hell upon the earth.

I haven't slept in more than a day but I've never felt more awake; my thinking and speech are somehow accelerated, and everything is being seared into my memory as if by the hand of God. If I close my eyes, I can still summon up the way that morning *smelled*—the sulfuric stench of gunpowder, the metallic tang of fresh blood, and the hellish, sickeningly sweet smell of roasting human flesh.

At the moment I'm on my horse in front of the Eldridge House, a four-story brick hotel at the corner of Fifth and Ohio streets, and I'm wearing my favorite red shirt—my battle shirt with the fancy stitching—and my gray trousers are tucked into a fine pair of tan cavalry boots. On my head is a black go-to-hell slouch hat with a turkey feather in the band. My favorite revolver, an 1860 Army, is tucked into my belt. It has a fluted cylinder and walnut grips, and the round barrel is more pleasing to my eyes than the octagonal muzzles of the smaller Navy Colts.

Also, I prefer the bigger punch of the .44-caliber ball.

Elsewhere on my person and slung by straps across the saddle are four other revolvers.

But I haven't fired a single one in anger yet, and I'm parlaying with Alexander Banks, the provost marshal of Kansas, who is in his nightshirt. Sleep has piled his wild hair atop his head, making a human exclamation point. Banks is standing impotently in the dirt street in front of me and I am towering over him; he is a man of normal height, but he must crane his head upward to talk to me. His nervous eyes are on a level with Old Charley's withers.

Old Charley is a dappled gray of fifteen hands and about twelve hundred pounds, and with a body like the boiler on a steam locomotive. Do you know much about horses? Old Charley is a blue horse, which means he was born solid black and his coat becomes progressively whiter as he ages; when I stole him near Paola, Kansas, before the war, he was three or four years old and a much darker gray. By the time I rode him into Lawrence, he had become a dappled gray.

Old Charley regards Banks with soft, dark eyes.

Banks, who lives in the hotel and has offices there, has been appointed by the occupants to ascertain my intent.

"Justice," I say. "Plunder."

"Those are rarely found together," Banks says indignantly.

"Ah, but when they are . . ." I say. "Would you sweeten the prize by resisting?"

Banks surrenders the hotel.

I tell him the building is to be looted, then destroyed.

Banks asks time for himself and the other guests to remove themselves. Feeling magnanimous, I agree—stipulating, of course, that the guests will be robbed first. Deciding to walk the halls of the hotel one last time before it is burned to the ground, I throw my reins to Honey John Noland, who is standing nearby cradling a .50-caliber Sharps carbine.

John allows the reins to drop in the mud. He is a muscular black man of thirty-five and has proved his courage and loyalty many times, but is a freeman and resentful of tasks he feels beneath him. He took the last name of his former masters, the brothers Bill and Hank Noland, when they freed him after the Jayhawkers burned their farm in Jackson County. They took to calling him Honey John because he had just about raised them, and was in the habit of calling them "honey." Others soon took it up to distinguish him in conversation from the other Johns among us: John Barker, John Graham, John Harris, John Koger, John McCorkle, John Ross.

"Colonel," Honey John asks me with disgust in his voice, "do I look like your stable nigger?"

"No, John. You are a freeman of color and a soldier."

"Then I am not here to hold your fucking horse."

Vess Akers, a redheaded kid with an old dragoon revolver stuck in his belt, steps forward grinning and snatches up the reins. At that moment a shirtless man with suspenders flopping comes tearing around the corner onto Ohio Street, and we can hear the sound of hooves behind him. He stumbles to a stop when he sees us. He is still thirty yards away, and his eyes are darting for a place to run. Vess cocks his head to one side, his red hair falling like a curtain over his left eye, and he pulls the big Walker pistol out of his waistband and flexes his arm in a smooth motion. Before his arm is fully extended the revolver barks and the barrel bucks upward, and a cloud of white powder smoke hangs a few feet in front of Vess. When it wafts away we can see the bare-chested man sprawled on the ground with a chunk of the left side of his head missing.

"You were off a little to the left," Honey John says.

Akers grins like a congenital idiot. He's still holding Old Charley's reins tightly in his left hand. Then the two riders who were chasing the shirtless man appear, regard their former prey for a moment, and then tear off down Fifth Street. One of them has a United States flag tied to the tail of his horse and it is dragging in the mud and is stained with horse shit.

Banks is staring at Honey John.

"What?" he demands.

"I know you," he said. "You were here, last week. You went door to door asking for work, and loafed in the alley behind the hotel. But you were really gathering names and addresses, weren't you?"

"Nobody pays much attention to a colored man, do they, suh?" Then John shifts the big Sharps to his other hand. "Not unless he's carrying a gun, that is."

"Don't you understand what this war is about?" Banks splutters.

"I do," Honey John says. "Don't you?"

I walk into the hotel and climb the stairs nearly to the second-floor landing, then turn so I can survey the lobby. A few frightened guests are huddled in one corner. On the floors above me, I can hear people milling about and talking in low anxious voices and the boots of the raiders thumping among them as the guests are relieved of their valuables.

"Charley Hart," a voice calls.

I look up and see an old acquaintance of mine, Arthur Spicer, leaning over the banister.

"I know you," he says brightly. "We used to spend our days together on the sandbar near the north ferry, shooting pistols and gambling. We drank, when we could get it. We called you Charley Hart then."

"It makes no difference," I say coolly.

"I just wanted to remind you—"

"It makes no difference," I repeat. "Do not speak to me again."

An old man dressed in black squeezes past Spicer to the landing. He is wearing trousers, but on his feet are nothing but stockings. He smoothes his coat, then addresses me.

"Are you—"

"Yes," I say. "Who are you?"

"David Bailey," he says. "I am a judge from Topeka."

"Your Honor," I ask, "where are your boots?"

"Stolen," he says. "Along with my money, except they left me enough for a dram of whiskey later. Now, see here, there are rumors that you are going to burn this hotel. That cannot be true."

"Indeed it is," I say.

"This is a heinous act that will not go unpunished," Bailey returns.

"This is punishment for a heinous act already committed," I say. "Do you not call that justice in your line of work?"

Then I tip my hat to the judge and step outside. I take the reins from Vess Akers and swing up into the saddle. After the guests are relocated and the hotel is blazing, I turn Old Charley and address my men. They have clustered around to watch the Eldridge House burn. I feel the weight of history bearing down upon my shoulders, and I think of Leonidas addressing the Spartans, of Caesar before he crossed the Rubicon, of Washington at Valley Forge.

But instead of a prayer, as Washington offered while kneeling in the snow, what comes from my mouth on this sweltering August morning is a curse.

"Kill!" I tell them. "Lawrence is to be cleansed, and the only way to accomplish that is with blood. They have made the spoon, and we shall make Jim Lane eat with it today! When in doubt, kill. Kill every man or boy capable of carrying a gun. Burn every home that flies the hated flag. Kill, and write your names in the blood of your victims upon the pages of history! Kill!"

You think me a monster now. So be it. But allow me to sketch the desperate events that led to the destruction of Lawrence, so that perhaps you will understand the context of such brutality.

A week earlier, the women's prison in Kansas City had collapsed. The Thomas House, a three-story brick building on Grand Avenue, had been pressed into use by the Federals, and many of the young women imprisoned on the second floor had committed no crime other than being related to the boys in my command. Some were wives and sweethearts, a few were sisters, some were cousins. Josephine Anderson, the sister of Bloody Bill, was killed during the collapse, and two other sisters were crippled; Charity Kerr, Cole Younger's cousin, also died. A pair of twin sisters, Susan and Armenia Crawford, were killed. A girl named Wilson also died. Of the two dozen survivors, all were grievously injured.

Rumors flew that the bastard Thomas Ewing—you'll have to forgive such language, for I will use it frequently

in this account—Ewing, a fellow Ohioan, and the commander of the Yankees in Kansas City, had weakened the
pillars in the basement in order to kill the women of the
guerrillas he so deeply despised. But by and by I heard
the real reason for the collapse, through my network of
spies, and it made Ewing seem almost gentle in comparison. The cellar was where the Yankees threw the whores
they had arrested, women who were drunks or drug ad-
dicts or so far gone with disease that they presented a
grave threat to public hygiene. But that didn't stop the
Yankee guards from knocking three great holes in the
common wall that separated the basement from their
quarters, so that they could get at the women, and the cellar became a working brothel. The women and the soldiers both were in such a degree of intoxication that they
did not notice the sagging joists, and axes were employed
to cut away even more columns to enlarge the operation.

When the building collapsed, I was engaged in a war
council in the Sni-A-Bar hills with the leaders of several
guerrilla bands, including Bloody Bill Anderson and
George Todd. I was attempting to convince them to hit
Lawrence, the Free State capital of the West, in retaliation for Jim Lane sacking and burning Osceola, Missouri,
the month before. My scouts had already gathered the
names and addresses of those to be targeted in Lawrence.
Among the addresses was the new two-story brick house
that bastard Lane had built for himself with plunder from
Osceola and a dozen other raids in Missouri.

But my fellow chieftains were hesitant, despite the
thousand injuries and insults that had been heaped upon
them and their families by the Yankee invaders. Lawrence
was forty miles inside the Kansas line, they said, and
even if we managed to raid the town, the odds were that
we'd never get back to Missouri alive.

But then news of the collapse of the women's prison in Kansas City came, and there was no more discussion. Between fits of tearing chunks of his hair from his head and beating the ground with his fists, Bill Anderson swore revenge and convinced the other lieutenants to do the same. The boys would ride, and I would lead them.

At the first sound of gunshots, Jim Lane had fled his fine new home in a state of partial dress and took refuge somewhere—a cornfield behind the house, perhaps, or suspended by a rope in a well. I never learned exactly where. When I arrive at his door, some of the boys are helping his wife, Mary, carry preserves from the cellar and stack them in the yard. They have been drinking a bit, and my lieutenant Jim Little is struggling beneath a double armload of preserves.

"What are you doing, Jimmie?" I ask from my horse.

"Colonel, we're helping the lady get her fruit and such out of the cellar, so that she'll have something to eat after we burn the house," he says. "That is, with the colonel's permission."

Then he drops one of the jars. It shatters on the ground, and Mary Lane clucks like an old hen.

"Is breaking jars all you're good for?" she asks.

"No, ma'am," Jim Little says. "I'm fair at breaking hearts as well."

Mary Lane stares at him with contempt.

"So, what do you say?" Jim Little asks. "Like to give it a whirl?"

His blue eyes are shining with stolen wine, and he strokes his silky mustache with the fingertips of his right hand in a gesture that seems suggestive, if not obscene. His beard is the same color as the hair on his head, which is to say deep brown, nearly black, and he wears his hair long, in the style of the frontier.

Like the other guerrillas, he is partial to anything with a rose design—the cut-down holster he wears on his belt has a rose stamped into the leather, and his hunting shirt is lousy with embroidered flowers and gathered with a rosette in front.

For these men, the rose is an icon of loyalty and secret fraternity, a symbol that identifies brothers in arms and confounds enemies. The rose is the heraldry employed in the "Wars of the Roses," a term coined by Sir Walter Scott in 1829 to refer to the English civil wars of the fifteenth century. The Missouri boys considered themselves "knights of the bush," and though most lacked an education and could not explicate its meaning, all knew the rose stood for things wonderful and mysterious.

The term "sub rosa" is Latin and means under the rose, and its origin goes back much further than Romans; the rose is the symbol of the Egyptian god Horus, worshipped as the god of silence. The rose later came to be associated with romance because the reckless affairs of the gods in Greek mythology were sealed in silence by the rose.

A rose given on Valentine's Day is not just a symbol of love; it is an invitation to secrecy. The roses that wives and sweethearts embroider on the hunting shirts of the men are their coats of arms, their manifestos, and their religions all rolled into one.

"Captain?" Jim Little asks.

"Yes?"

"You were asleep in the saddle," he says. "With your eyes open."

"Lost in thought," I said.

"Drunk is more like it," Mary Lane says. "You ruffians

think you're something special, don't you? Well, you'll never be half the man my senator is."

"I'll give you that," Jim Little says, and smiles broadly. "I know for damned sure that none of us have stolen even half as much as your old man."

"There's a piano in the parlor that I would like to get out of the house," Mrs. Lane says. "That is, if you can be a little more careful with it than you are with those preserves."

"I'm not sure this is working toward our objective," I tell the boys. "Taking everything out of the house before setting the torch to it takes some of the sting out of the act, don't you think?"

"Well, I hadn't thought of it from that angle," Jim Little says.

"And don't you think the time you're spending on this housework could be better spent *looking* for Jim Lane?" I ask. "He can't have gotten too far, do you think?"

Jim Little looks at his feet.

"Thank God you blackguards haven't found the senator," Mrs. Lane says. "No doubt you would have shot him dead."

"No, madam," I say, and remove my slouch hat. "It was my intention to haul him back to Jackson County, give him a fair trial on charges of murder, arson, and theft, and then to hang him."

"You shall never catch him," Mrs. Lane vows.

"Give Senator Lane my compliments," I say. "Tell him I was looking forward to meeting him."

"I'm sure he would be glad to make your acquaintance," she says, "but under more favorable circumstances."

"Make sure you fire the house, boys," I say.

Then I turn my horse and ride back through the chaos

toward the center of town. There is so much going on that you can only take in what is happening in one neighborhood at a time; here a group of men with revolvers drawn chase a resident through a vegetable garden, there one of the boys strides out of a house with a jug tucked beneath one arm and his pockets full of silver, there a blackened corpse lies half in the flames of what was once a trim wood house.

It is grim, I tell myself, but it is war.

And then I come upon something unnerving.

It is the body of a boy, perhaps fifteen, faceup in the street with arms and legs bent at joint-busting angles. He has taken a ball from a rifle squarely in the forehead, and his brains have dribbled out the back of his skull. He has been trod upon several times by the horses of the raiders. The boy is dressed in the checked wool shirt of a laborer, and he's missing his trousers and one of his shoes. The pink toes of his left foot are smeared with mud. His lower abdomen has been crushed, and his manhood displaced. His neck has a gash so large that it exposes the gleaming white jawbone.

Two large and very black crows are perched atop his chest, teasing stringy bits of flesh from the neck wound. A mangy yellow dog is sniffing and slobbering over the insult to his groin.

I nudge Charley forward, and the crows protest and flap their wings, and hop away from the body. Finally, they take flight. The dog, however, is reluctant to yield. The dog snarls as I urge Old Charley closer. Charley dislikes dogs and he approaches in a sideways prance, bobbing his head vigorously to express his displeasure.

I pull the Army from my belt.

The dog snarls.

I cock and fire in one motion. The ball strikes the dog

in the side of the chest and knocks him yelping backward. Then the dog tries to stand, eyes soft and wide and its muzzle still wet with human blood. I thumb back the hammer again, aim, and place the next round into the dog's eye.

Whatever restraints that keep men from behaving as beasts have been slipped this day in Lawrence. You've probably heard the now-famous qualification that we treated women well, but I can put the lie to that. While we did not assault their persons, we savaged their spirits. I'm sure many of the women and girls would have chosen death over witnessing the grim events of that Friday morning. The catalog of horrors are on such a scale as to be unknown to any single human being, and if painstakingly collected by a team of scholars, would take many volumes to index.

And my exhortation to *kill, kill*?

I feel neither proud nor ashamed, but regard it as a curious artifact of a time long past—a clue to another life, evidence of a passion long lost, a communiqué very nearly from the other side of the grave. What men may think of me is no longer of concern; the dread judge waits upon the far shore.

Now, don't ask me to describe what unnerved me so about the crows feasting upon the dead boy; while that image is grim enough, there is another forever burned into my memory. Even if there were words to convey the horror, I dare not speak of it. And while I have attempted to forget about it every day since, the image is always waiting for me, appearing just as I'm about to drift off to sleep, jolting me awake as surely as a pistol shot.

When it was over, Lawrence was reduced to ashes and two hundred men and boys lay dead. It was a stunning victory, one of only two the South had in the West in 1863; I was also responsible for the other, the defeat of the swarthy little bastard Blunt at Baxter Springs a few weeks later. Yet I received no triumph; no laurels was I offered.

Instead, I was called a monster—or the devil.

From the day of the Lawrence raid forward, I was on the run. If I wasn't running from the Yankees, I was running from my murderous comrades, and if I wasn't running from them, I was running from myself—or some version thereof.

Now I can run no longer.

For whenever I close my eyes to sleep, it is always seven o'clock in the morning on Friday, August 21, 1863, at Lawrence, along the banks of the Kaw in northeastern Kansas, beneath a full moon in the morning sky—and I am the architect of the unspeakable.

Book One

There were three ravens sat on a tree,
Downe a downe, hay downe, hay downe
There were three ravens sat on a tree,
With a downe
There were three ravens sat on a tree,
There were as black as they might be.
With a downe, derrie, derrie, downe, downe

> —The Three Ravens, *traditional ballad*
> *(Collected 1611)*

A Better Fate

I was born William Clarke Quantrill twenty-seven years ago at Canal Dover, Ohio, but even this simple bit of biography would confuse my closest companions; most have known me as the border ruffian Charley Hart or sometimes Captain Clarke, of either the Rebel or Federal armies, depending upon need and inclination. All suppose that I was born in Kentucky, and even those few to whom I have confided my given name can spell it no better than the editors of Yankee newspapers. Many don't even try, finding it easier, as I indicated earlier, to simply call me the devil.

As an aside, let me say that I am confident that you will not make the same mistake regarding my name. As to whether I am truly the devil of my own story, or merely an associate, you are left to your own conclusions.

Had I more time I would give a full accounting of my family's pedigree all the way back to Adam, tell an amusing but illuminating story about my boyhood that involves a school-yard bully and a lesson dealt, and bring you to tears over the last time I saw my loving old mother. But time is among the many damned things I do not have, for reasons that shall become clear, so I will start very near the end.

I quit Missouri in December, after having gathered thirty or forty of the boys one last time in Lafayette County in north central Missouri. And when I call them "boys," I mean it—most were not yet twenty. A few weren't shaving yet. But all of them were related in some degree to one another; if they weren't brothers, they were cousins, and if they weren't actually joined by blood, then they were related by marriage. And if they weren't kin by either blood or law, then they were united by geography or inclination.

By the time the boys gathered for the last time in Fayette County, the card cheat George Todd lay dead, having been shot through the neck and killed while engaging in some trivial skirmish near Independence, and the berserker Bill Anderson had been cut down after being fool enough to ride into an ambush in Ray County. Anderson's head was hacked from his body and placed on a telegraph pole, to the delight of the troopers who had found Yankee scalps hanging from the bridle of his horse.

I felt no sorrow at the passing of either Todd or Bloody Bill, because both had betrayed me in Texas, and history will record that their leadership was as brief as it was unremarkable; everything of note that either did was accomplished under my command. Yet, I would be less than truthful if I denied a certain chilling effect their deaths had upon me. Once, both had been my friends.

And the war, of course, was lost.

With Lee's defeat at Gettysburg and the fall of Vicksburg within just a day of each other in July 1863, the Confederacy was doomed. Out West, Old Pap Price had raised hell in Missouri, but didn't take St. Louis when he had the chance in the fall of '64. After touring the whole damned state and scrapping three or four dozen times, the Yankees finally drove Old Pap back to the Red River.

So the only choice left for me and the boys to make was where to finish the fight. We had given no quarter and expected none, had been part of no regular army, and after the burning of Lawrence and the victory at Baxter Springs had been hunted like wild beasts. The Federal authorities had declared us outlaws and that we were to be shot on sight or, if captured, summarily hanged; our reign in Missouri was over.

Some of the fellows were in favor of going to Texas, where in the old days we had wintered at the Mineral Creek Camp south of the Red River. From Texas, we could cross the Rio Grande into Mexico and thus be far from the reach of Yankee laws. But living in exile held no appeal for me, and instead I suggested we relocate; I didn't know where, as long as it was anywhere else than Missouri. I was even entertaining the notion of striking out for Washington with a handful of men and assassinating that bastard Abraham Lincoln.

But it didn't turn out that way.

I am often reminded now of the letter I received at Mineral Creek from Tom Reynolds, Confederate governor of Missouri exiled to the state of Texas. I had offered to raise four hundred Missouri partisans who had refused service in the regular army but who would join any campaign to retake Missouri. The governor replied that I should join the regular army and give up my dark command, and I can yet quote the conclusion of the governor's letter:

A man of your ability should look forward to a higher future. All authority over undisciplined bands is short-lived. The history of every guerrilla chief has been the same. My opinion of you is that you deserve a better fate, and should rise higher than you now stand.

Now, to stand at all would be enough.

A Hard Winter

A week later we were in the middle of the state in one of the hardest winters any of us could remember. The weather was so bad that most of the Yankees were holed up, which allowed us free movement, and the odd patrol we did encounter just took a look at our stolen uniforms and waved in greeting.

We waved back.

At Tuscumbia, a little town on the Osage River about thirty miles southwest of Jefferson City, we discovered by chance that the local militia was quartered in the city's hotel. We drew up to the hotel at about seven o'clock in the morning and found a cadaverous corporal huddled in a blanket and clutching a tin cup of coffee. When he saw the bars on my shoulder straps he threw off the blanket and jumped to his feet, spilling the coffee in the process and cursing beneath his breath.

"Corporal," I called from the saddle after returning his salute. "Does your commander allow you to stand your duty while wrapped in a blanket like a red Indian?"

"No, sir," the soldier said. "Begging the captain's pardon, but I've been feeling a bit punk this morning."

"You look feverish," I said.

"A cold," he said. "It will pass, sir."

I removed my gloves, and then used them to slap the trail dust from my blue frock coat. Old Charley shifted beneath me. He used to be as solid as if he were made of wood instead of horseflesh, but in the last year or so had taken to favoring his right front hoof, which he would hold ever so lightly above the ground. He was eight years old now. His coat had turned even lighter, from dappled gray to nearly white with brown flecks—a color sometimes called flea-bitten, a term I despised.

"It is my desire to pay my respects to the post commander," I said.

Behind me, the boys looked bored but were busy eyeballing every window and door in sight.

"Captain Applewaith is headquartered in the white house on the hill," the corporal said.

"Where's the rest of the garrison?"

"Here in the hotel."

"All of them?"

"It's a small garrison," he said. "Less than company strength. Sixty or so."

I nudged Old Charley forward.

"Captain?"

"What is it?"

"I must have your papers," the thin corporal said. "Sorry, sir, but those are my orders. The bushwhackers have taken to posing as Union soldiers, you know. Todd and Anderson are dead, but Quantrill is still on the loose. . . ."

"Do I look like a bushwhacker to you, Corporal?" I asked.

"No, sir," he said, stammering a bit. "But my orders . . ."

"Good man," I said and reached inside my jacket. I

produced a commission, still bound with a red ribbon, that I had taken from the body of a dead Yankee a year or so before and handed it down to the corporal. While he struggled to undo the ribbon, I looked over the town.

Not so much as a dog was moving on the dirt street.

Smoke curled from the limestone chimneys at either end of the hotel, there was the creak of leather as the boys shifted in their saddles, and every few moments there came a sharp *whack* as somebody split wood at the edge of town. I remember sitting easily in the saddle as the thin corporal read the commission, and reflecting on how it seemed the most natural thing in the world to ride into a town held by the enemy and begin to bluff or force our way to what we desired. God knows we'd done it enough in the last five years.

The corporal folded the commission, tied a clumsy knot, and handed it up.

"And your orders?"

"Secret," I said. "But I will present Captain Applewaith with a letter authorizing any Federal troops we encounter to render us whatever aid is practical. Have you recently been supplied, Corporal?"

"Oh yes, sir," the corporal said. "Steam packet came to the landing just yesterday with blankets and ammunition and victuals. No more hardtack for a spell—we have eggs and bacon and canned pears."

"What a delight for you."

"Captain Clarke," the corporal asked, ignoring my insult, "may I have the honor of introducing you to Captain Applewaith?"

"Tend to your duties here," I said. "But it would be a kindness if you could share the source of your coffee with my men."

"Right away, sir."

"Lieutenant," I said, turning in the saddle to address Jim Little, who wore a uniform with the appropriate rank. "Accompany me to the captain's headquarters. Sergeant Glasscock, you're in charge."

Dick Glasscock smiled broadly. He was one of the older men, in his late twenties. His head was shaved and the blouse he wore was a bit too small—the buttons over his hard round stomach looked as if they might pop. Hanging from his belt was an Arkansas toothpick, a knife with an eighteen-inch blade and a heavy brass guard.

"Salute, damn you," I said.

"Sorry, sir."

Glasscock threw me the worst salute in the history of any army, a wild gesture with his left hand that began someplace near his brow and ended somewhere at his side.

"I won't dignify that sorry attempt at a salute," I said. "Keep working on distinguishing your left from your right, Sergeant."

"Right you are," Glasscock replied.

Then he grinned, revealing a row of sharp yellow teeth that made him resemble a white cannibal. But then, I've read that cannibals never kill more than they can eat.

"Sir," Glasscock said, "are you going to tell us some more stories about the old days? About knights and desperate battles and terrible revenge? Why, I've got a mind to make some more angels out of—"

"That's enough," I told him.

Once, I had made the mistake of telling Glasscock about a particularly grim method of execution called the blood eagle. For the thousandth time, I wished I had not shared this bit of history.

"Dismount," I called. "And mind your manners. Smoke, drink coffee, but no gambling and no swearing. I suggest this is a good time to read your Bibles or to write letters to your families at home, but mind the horses and be ready to move on short notice."

I swung down from Old Charley and threw the reins to Clark Hockensmith, who caught them in a broad hand even though he wasn't looking in my direction at the time.

"Treat that horse as you would your dearest friend," I said.

"My dearest friend ran off with my first wife," Hockensmith said. "Do you want me to beat this animal before or after I—"

"That will do, soldier," I said.

The thin corporal tugged at his color and cleared his throat, and finally got up the nerve to speak.

"If'n you don't mind me asking, sir . . ."

"Speak, Corporal."

"Where you boys from?" he asked.

"Colorado Territory," I said.

"Well, you sure have a peculiar idea of discipline in Colorado," he said, spitting as he talked. "If I talked like that to my commander, he'd have me skinned, and I'd have it coming."

"Corporal," I said, "how many times in the heat of battle have you saved your captain's life?"

"Well, I reckon . . ."

"I thought so," I said. "Look over these men, soldier. Most of them have saved my skin at one time or another. And a few times, I've saved theirs."

The corporal was confused.

"May I ask what battles the captain and his troops have been engaged in?" he asked. "I am unaware of any Colorado outfit—"

"No," I said. "The corporal may not."

As we walked up the path to the house, Jim Little was chortling with delight.

"Bill," he said, "you get better at this every time."

Jim Little now walked with a limp. He'd been shot through the hips at the Fayette fight in September of '64 when the fool Anderson was attempting to take a blockhouse with a cavalry charge. I had wheeled Old Charley about and rode back into the fire and drew Jim Little up into the saddle with me. Luck was with me, because with a wounded man in one arm and the reins in the other, I was unable to fire a single shot to cover our retreat. Anderson damned me for a fool and said that had I not rode in to rescue a dead man, the assault would not have faltered, but to hell with that. For a while, though, I wondered if I hadn't truly risked my life for a corpse. Nobody expected Jim Little to live when we dropped him off at his cousin's house near Lexington, because he'd also been hit in the right arm and was bleeding badly, but when the call went out in December, he was waiting for us, horse saddled and guns capped. When he asked to shake my hand, I was shocked to discover that the middle finger of his right hand was missing, having been shot off in the Fayette fight.

"Don't worry, Colonel," he said. "It ain't my trigger finger and it doesn't affect my aim, although a Navy fits my hand a might easier than the big Remington I used to favor."

"It's captain again, Jimmie," I said. "Colonel was a brevet rank. I'm back to my old commission in the partisan rangers."

"It could be colonel or captain or even Quantrill the private soldier," Jim Little had said. "Whatever it is, I'll follow you through the gates of hell, even though shooting our way back out might be a bit rough."

The house was one of those ornate affairs with wood trim that reminded me of the filigree on a steamboat, and it probably belonged to the local judge or perhaps was the home of a pilot who had made a fortune before the war. We paused on the porch for a moment and looked each other over before pounding on the door to announce ourselves.

"Your hat," I told Jim Little, indicating his battered slouch hat. "Rake it a bit. Ah, just so."

"You enjoy this playacting, don't you, Bill?"

"I enjoy a very many things," I said. "But yes, had fate conspired to give me another life, I think I would like to have trod the boards. Or been a poet. I am a great admirer of Lord Byron, and can quote him at length. But there's a heart for every fate, as old George said, and this heart—and this fate—are my own."

Jim Little stared at me in amazement.

"You are the damnedest thing I ever saw," he said finally.

That Devil Quantrill

Jim Little pounded on the door with his gloved fist. He waited a few seconds, then began to pound again, with more urgency. Then the door swung open, and a startled first lieutenant was looking at Jim Little's upraised fist.

"What's your meaning?"

"Our meaning was to get your attention," I said, stepping past the lieutenant into the parlor. "Where is Captain Applewaith?"

"Taking breakfast in his bedroom upstairs," the adjutant said.

"Fetch him," I said.

"I beg your pardon," the lieutenant said.

"That wasn't a request, son," I said. "We're in a damned hurry because of a desperate band of guerrillas known to be in the area."

The lieutenant bounded up the stairs, and in a few moments the rumored Captain Applewaith came down while tucking his shirttails into his breeches. A few biscuit crumbs remained in his beard. The lieutenant was on his heels, whispering in his ear, but when Applewaith reached the bottom of the stairs he held up his hand for silence.

Without speaking, I withdrew the commission and offered it. Applewaith took it, undid the ribbon, and carefully read the document.

"Captain Clarke of the Second Colorado," he said. "Hensley tells me you are chasing guerrillas."

I nodded.

"Are they near?"

"Very," I said.

"Which band?" Applewaith asked as he walked into the parlor and motioned for me to follow. He went to a side table beneath a military map of the Trans-Mississippi West and opened a wooden box that held cigars stacked like cordwood.

I took one of the cigars he offered and bit the end off. "Hard to say."

"Could it be that devil Quantrill?" he asked.

I watched Applewaith for a few long seconds, studying the fear in his eyes.

"I'm afraid so."

Then he struck a Lucifer match and held it beneath the cigar while I puffed life into it. He took a cigar for himself and lit it, then ordered Lieutenant Hensley to fetch three glasses of brandy.

"Do you have whiskey?" I asked.

"Of course," Applewaith said. "But it's seven o'clock in the morning."

"The whiskey, if you please," I said. "We've been riding for a long spell in the bitter cold."

Applewaith instructed Hensley to get the whiskey, then explained that the owner was quite fond of Kentucky whiskey and always kept a few earthenware jugs hidden in the cellar.

"Not hidden well enough," I said. "Where is the master of the house? I'd like to thank him for his hospitality."

"Sleeping comfortably, I trust," he said. "Old Man Evans was a widower and childless who died of the smallpox a few weeks ago. He's in the cemetery out back."

"Shame," I said. "I would have toasted his health."

"Smallpox?" Jim Little asked.

"Yes, unfortunately," the captain said. "It came down the river and spread like wildfire. Took half the company before the infection was finally stopped by burning clothing and blankets. And the medical cure was worse than the disease. I think the doctors killed more men with their damned vaccinations than the disease took."

"The vaccinations?" Jim Little asked.

"Oh, you've never seen it?" Applewaith asked. "Well, being from Colorado Territory, you wouldn't have, I suppose. Our modern doctor takes the scabs from a victim, slashes the arm of a healthy man, and then rubs the scabs into the resulting wound. A ghastly sight when it begins to fester."

Jim Little made a face.

"I know how you feel," Applewaith said, then turned the conversation back to me. "Captain Clarke, anything we can do to assist you in bringing these outlaws to justice—preferably at the end of a rope—is at your disposal."

"What we need most desperately is someone to lead us across the Osage and to points east, since we are quite unfamiliar with this country."

"Consider it done," Applewaith said. "Private Jackson grew up on a farm on the far side of the river and knows these bottoms as well as any man alive. He is also an excellent scout and can follow sign like a red Indian. Wherever the guerrillas may have gone, he can lead you to them."

"Jackson," I said.

"Yes, Thomas Jefferson Jackson," the captain said. "I am, of course, anxious to assist you, but I'm suffering a touch of gout which renders me incapable of riding for any distance. I'm sure you understand."

"Perfectly," I said.

At this point, Hensley appeared with a tray that contained three generous glasses of an amber brown liquid.

"This isn't popskull, I trust."

"No," Applewaith reassured me. "Bourbon from Kentucky. Corn liquor. Aged in oak and not an ounce of peat. Some say it's the finest in the world, and I'm inclined to agree. Please, help yourselves."

Jim Little and I each took a glass, and Applewaith took the third. He waited until we had taken a drink before he took a sip of his own. The liquor tasted of oak and charcoal and a bit of caramel. But it burned all the way down my throat, and then it was like a live shell had exploded in my stomach and was radiating fire through my torso.

Jim Little coughed, and wiped his mouth with his sleeve.

"Good Lord," he said.

"Water of life," Applewaith said.

"Pardon?" Jim Little asked, still coughing.

"That's what whiskey means in Gaelic," Applewaith said.

"Gaelic?"

"The native language of Ireland," I said. "I know a little of it; my father was a tinker, and as such was privy to the secret language of tinkers, which includes a smattering of Gaelic."

I noticed that Applewaith was staring at my waist, so I asked what was commanding his attention.

"Your sash, sir," Applewaith said, motioning with his cigar hand toward my wine-colored sash. "It is striking."

"Thank you."

"The tassels are distinctive, as are the embroidery and the richness of the color," he said. Smoke curled from the cigar in his right hand. In his left was the glass of whiskey. "I don't think I've seen another like it, except perhaps for the one General Blunt's adjutant used to wear."

"The tassels *are* rather large," I said. "But I prefer them that way. The way the pair hangs has always struck me as decidedly . . . masculine."

"Indeed," the idiot went on. "The adjutant was Major Henry Curtis, the son of General Sam Curtis. He was killed and robbed . . . he was robbed of his sash . . ."

"Yes, Captain?"

Applewaith cleared his throat.

"He was robbed of it at Baxter Springs by Quantrill," he said, frowning. He cast down his eyes, swirled the whiskey in his glass, and took a drink for courage. "You're he, aren't you?"

When he glanced back up he was looking at the barrel of my Army revolver, which I had drawn from my sash and which was now held casually in my left hand. The captain, who had been in the process of dressing as he came down the stairs to meet us, was not wearing a sidearm.

Jim Little reached out and took the lieutenant's pistol from its holster and pointed it at its former owner, who had closed his eyes and was making water in his trousers.

"Hensley, you've disgraced yourself," Applewaith observed.

"Yes, sir," the lieutenant said, eyes still closed.

Jim Little swore and stepped back as the puddle widened.

"For God's sake," Applewaith said. "If they were going to kill us, they would have done so by now. So open your eyes and regard the architect of the destruction of Lawrence."

"No, sir," Hensley said. "Thank you, sir."

I took the stinking cigar from my mouth and threw it into the fireplace.

"Take a look," Applewaith urged again, and then he drained the last of his whiskey and took a puff from the cigar. "Here's the monster that in the fall of 1863 reduced Lawrence, the Free State capital of Kansas, to a blazing funeral pyre for hundreds of unarmed men and boys and made the muddy Kaw run red with blood."

"They was unarmed because they were so damned stupid they passed a law that a private citizen couldn't carry a firearm within the city limits," Jim Little said. "They had plenty of guns, but they had 'em all locked up in the armory. And they all deserved what they got because of that thieving Jim Lane and our women what was killed in the collapse of the prison at Kansas City."

Applewaith ignored him.

"A fortnight later, this fiend massacred a hundred Union soldiers under the command of General Blunt at Baxter Springs. He was at the head of his column of brigands wearing a blue uniform, just as he is now, and the general believed it was a welcoming party sent out from Fort Blair. The general even put his regimental band out front. The musicians were killed, right down to the twelve-year-old drummer boy. The general escaped, thank God, but was forced to abandon the mule-drawn wagon that carried his personal effects, including his dress sword, letters of commission, and the headquarters flag that was painstakingly sewn by the ladies of Leavenworth."

"It wasn't a massacre," Jim Little said. "It was a battle. And it wasn't our fault because Blunt was ignorant enough to line his men up so we could knock 'em down."

"So that is your excuse for murder," Applewaith said. "What would be your excuse for scalping?"

Jim Little turned his revolver from the quaking lieutenant and trained it upon the captain.

"Bill, let me bust a cap on this one just to shut him up," Jim Little said as he cocked the revolver. He held the gun a little awkwardly on account of the missing finger, and for a moment I was afraid he would lose his grip or that the gun would go off by accident.

But Applewaith ignored the cocked revolver.

"Open your eyes, Hensley, and behold the devil."

Hensley's eyes blinked open.

"I assure you, Lieutenant, there is more to the story," I said.

The whiskey had made me a bit sleepy, and gave the scene a peculiar and pleasant warmth. For a moment I had trouble following what had last been said—oh yes, Applewaith had called me the devil, and I had allowed there was more to the story, but I didn't feel inclined to explain it. But then I thought of Blunt, and I turned to Applewaith, still puffing on his damned cigar.

"Do you know where that swarthy little bastard is now?"

"Who?" he asked.

"Blunt," I said. "Do you know of any other swarthy little bastards?"

"I hardly think General Blunt is swarthy and I certainly do not regard him as a bastard," Applewaith said.

"I do not know where the general is at present, but if I did, I would not tell."

"As you wish," I said.

"What are your demands?"

"Breakfast for the boys," I said. "All of your arms and ammunition. Blankets, overcoats, India-rubber ponchos. Socks. Boots, certainly. What money you have, especially if it is in gold or silver coin. The scout you mentioned, Jackson."

Applewaith hesitated.

"Is that all?"

"Maps. Everything you have. And newspapers," I said. "Anything at all, whether it is recent or not. Gather them up now, for I will be taking breakfast with my men at the hotel, and you shall have the pleasure of accompanying me."

Later, on our walk back to the hotel, it began to rain. As we marched along, with Applewaith and his cowardly lieutenant before us, our guns kept hidden but ready beneath our coats, Jim Little grinned and asked if there could be any business that provided as much pure joy as bushwhacking.

"If there is," I allowed, "it ought to be a crime."

Fat Children!

As we neared the hotel, the thin corporal struggled to his feet. His great long face was flushed and shone with sweat, despite the cold. He held a salute as we mounted the steps.

"No need for that," Applewaith said.

The corporal lowered his hand.

"This man behind me is in charge now," Applewaith said. "Comply with his demands, as long as they are humane, but offer him neither salute nor any other sign of respect you would ordinarily extend to an officer."

"Sir?"

I produced the revolver from beneath my coat.

"Oh, so that's how it is," the corporal said. "I knew there was something peculiar about you Colorado boys."

"They're not from Colorado, you imbecile," Applewaith blustered.

"Take it easy," I told Applewaith. "Act like nothing's the matter. Laugh, as if I just told you the best joke you've heard all week. That's it. Now tell me where the company keeps the armory."

"In the back room off the pantry," the corporal said. "It

was the only room we could find with a decent lock. Sergeant Harlan has the key on a chain around his neck."

"Where's this Harlan now?"

"Saw him a while ago making his way to the landing. Said he was searching for a case of canned pears that somehow didn't make it from the packet boat to the hotel."

"Bill," Jim Little called.

He was standing close to Hensley, but his dark eyes were fixed on a clump of blue figures in the yard beyond the porch, stacking firewood in the rain. Beyond them, another squad was throwing some tarps over the bed of a wagon.

"When we got here, it seemed like all of the Yankees were holed up in the hotel trying to keep warm," he said. "Now that it's raining, they all seem to have chores. What now?"

I called to Joe Hall, who was sitting cross-legged on the porch, a carbine across his lap and the blanket that had formerly been worn by the thin corporal across his shoulders.

"Find the drummer," I said. "Tell him the captain has asked him to call assembly."

Joe tossed the blanket aside and ran into the hotel.

Sweat dripped from the tip of the corporal's chin and darkened the neck of his shirt. His legs must also have been weak because he was swaying like a pendulum.

"Are you scared?" I asked.

"No, sir," he said. "Must have been sicker than I thought."

"Sit down before you fall down," I said.

"Thank you," he said.

"Don't speak," I said. "And don't touch anything or anyone."

Jim Little regarded the corporal with contempt. "He's got the smallpox."

"We don't know for sure," I said.

"We ought to shoot the sonuvabitch anyway," he said.

"We'll lock him in a room by himself," I said.

In five minutes the drummer had tapped out the rhythm for assembly and the company materialized like ghosts in the rain. My boys surrounded them as I explained their situation. We had them march right military-like by the wagon, where we had them throw whatever weapons they had into the bed. There were rifles and bayonets and a few pistols. Then we marched them into the hotel and packed them into the big room on the ground floor, where it would be easy to keep an eye on all of them.

But we kept the cook and his helper busy in the kitchen.

While I waited on my ham and eggs, I went to the room off the pantry and examined the lock.

"Where's the sergeant with that key?"

"Haven't found him," Jim Little said. "For all we know, he might have fallen in the river looking for that damned case of pears."

"Get an ax," I said.

Hockensmith fetched the ax from the woodpile and then delighted in reducing the door to splinters. I kicked my way through what was left and, while hoping to find a crate of Colt revolvers or Spencer carbines, discovered instead two neat rows of Springfields. The Springfield is the standard Federal infantry weapon, and while it throws a .58-caliber Minié ball nearly a mile, it is a long and clumsy weapon and worse than useless for a mounted soldier.

"Throw the Springfields in the wagon," I told Hockensmith. "Go over the room and take anything that looks interesting."

Then I went to the dining room to take breakfast.

Breakfast, of course, is the best part of any guerrilla raid.

I cannot recommend the forced breakfast strongly enough, particularly if you find yourself in any middling village early some morning in Kansas or Missouri. Firstly, it scares the hell out of your enemy, because having the *dash* to demand breakfast and then to eat it at your *leisure* is a testament to your total command of the situation; secondly, you're probably hungry, having ridden a good distance and possibly in bad weather; and thirdly— and this is the most important—it calms the nerves and gives you time to think about your next move.

The table was set, a fire blazed in the hearth, and the curtains were drawn back to allow a good view of the street. Jim Little was lounging in a chair near the window, keeping watch, and Applewaith sat stiffly in the corner, arms folded across his chest. Hensley sat next to him, the pile of maps and charts on his lap.

Vess Akers, one of the youngest boys, was sitting guard next to him.

Vess had a tangle of hair the color of ripe pumpkins, his clothes were homespun, and his shirt had been sewn by his mother, who thrust him into my care one Sunday afternoon after she learned his brother, Stu, had died somewhere in the Ozarks. I attempted to decline the responsibility, concerned that Sylvester Akers was too young, but Mother Akers said she could no longer feed her surviving child and that he should learn to kill Yankees.

The old dragoon pistol Vess carried had probably seen service in the Mexican War. It weighed five pounds, had a barrel that was eight inches long, and was stained dark brown by a couple decades of rust and grease and spent gunpowder. I had urged him to adopt a lighter and newer weapon, but he declined, and soon demonstrated that he was a frightfully good shot with the antique, even from horseback. An added advantage was that the Walker packed as much powder and lead in each of its long chambers as some rifles. When Vess shot a Yankee with it, the Yankee seldom got back up.

I drew a chair up to the table and asked for the newspapers.

Jim Little took them from Applewaith and placed them at my elbow. Meanwhile, the cook's assistant came and filled a real china cup with steaming coffee, which I cooled a bit with cream from an earthenware pitcher. The newspapers were a mix of the local *Miller County Autogram*, the *New Madrid Semi-Weekly Earthquake*, and various St. Louis City publications.

"Listen to this, Jimmie," I called while regarding a page from the *Dispatch*. " 'Fat children! Those among our readers who love fat babies should call upon Colonel Grimm at Third Street near Washington. He is exhibiting there a Dutch boy who is but twelve years of age but whose girth measures five feet and four and one-half inches. The girl, of uncertain ancestry, is six years of age, measures four and one-half feet about the waist.' "

Vess thought a moment about this.

"It seems to me," he said, "that if a man took the time to learn how to read, he would want to fill his mind with the important things. Like reading the Bible."

"Bored the hell out of me," I said.

"Is there no news of the war?" Jim Little asked. "Give me the damned papers."

"There is, and we shall get to it by and by," I said. "But

first let us laugh at the paid notices, which are snags for the gullible. Here's something worthy of particular note from the *Earthquake*: 'Dr. Kelso, the king of cancer doctors, has located his office and residence on the Levee Road near Main, where the afflicted can be assured of a safe and certain cure. He is the only doctor living that can kill and extract a cancer in twenty-four hours, without instruments, pain, or the loss of a drop of blood; and he challenges the world to produce remedies equal to his in curing diseases of the spine, including paralysis, whether the cause is congenital or due to injury.' "

"Is such a thing truly possible?" Vess asked.

"They couldn't print it if it weren't true," I said.

"Do you think this doctor might cure Jim's leg?" Vess asked with hope in his voice. "I notice that the colder it gets, the more it seems to trouble him. Perhaps the doctor could make him walk like he used to before the blockhouse fight."

"Don't worry about me," Jim Little said. "The leg don't hurt; I just drag it sometimes because I'm lazy."

"Should we ever find ourselves near the village of New Madrid," I told Vess, "we'll have to pay a visit to this Dr. Kelso and put his claims to the test."

"The war news," Jim Little pressed.

I leafed through the papers.

"It's not good," I said. "Hood has been crushed at Nashville. Sherman was closing on Atlanta, or at least he was as of a week ago."

Then I fell silent as I scanned the other news. Of particular interest was the situation in Kentucky, a formerly neutral border state where anti-Union sentiment was exploding. The bastard Lincoln had declared martial law and Yankee General Stephen Burbridge had issued general orders that captured guerrillas would no longer be treated as prisoners of war, but would be immediately subject to imprisonment and probable execution.

On an inside page of the *Dispatch* I found an item that had been relayed by telegraph from the *Louisville Journal*, under the headline FEMALE GUERRILLA STEALING MORE THAN HEARTS IN NORTH CENTRAL KENTUCKY.

"Jimmie, this one's about a band of partisans in Kentucky," I said. "It's about a raid where they tried to rob a bank but was surprised by the home guard, but get this: 'One of the peculiarities of this band of cutthroats is the officer second in command . . . a young woman, and her right name is Sue Mundy. She dresses in male attire, generally sporting a full Confederate uniform. She is possessed of a comely form, is a bold rider and a dashing leader.'"

"A comely form?" Vess asked.

"Curvy," I explained, then continued reading: "'The lieutenant is a practiced robber, and many ladies, who have been so unfortunate as to meet her on the highway, can testify with what sangfroid she presents a pistol and commands "Stand and deliver."'"

"What's . . . san . . . sandfrog . . . whatever the hell you said."

"Sangfroid," I repeated. "It's a fancy word that means cold-blooded."

"Huh?"

"Cool under fire. Calm. Brave."

"Keep reading," Vess urged.

"'Her name is becoming widely known, and associated with horror. On Friday evening she robbed a stage outside Harrodsburg and relieved a young lady of her watch and chain.' And that's all it says about the female guerrilla."

"How far is Kentucky?" Vess asked.

"Let's take a look," I said. "Hensley, give us a map. And make sure it's a dry one. I can't stand the stench of urine."

Hensley shuffled through his stack of maps and charts and finally found a general map of the United States and fortunately, it was dry. Unfolded, it occupied most of the tabletop, and I had to move my coffee.

"Here's Kentucky," I said, pointing to the protean shape to the east. "See, the narrow western tip just touches the Missouri boot heel here, or would if the Mississippi weren't in between; that's the near part and it's about three hundred miles distant."

"Where is the lady guerrilla with the cold blood?"

"Oh, she's much farther away," I said. I found Louisville on the Ohio River and then moved my finger down to the middle of the state. "She's in these hills, some four or maybe five hundred miles from here."

I left my finger in north-central Kentucky, but my eyes followed the Ohio River to the northeast, then up the canal system into Ohio and finally to a dot in Tuscarawas County with the diminutive legend CANAL DOVER.

"It would take us three weeks or a month of hard riding to get there in this weather," I said in a low voice, to avoid sharing intelligence with Applewaith and the sniveling Hensley. "But it's an interesting thought, isn't it?"

Jim Little leaned close and whispered, "You can't be considering . . ."

"Do you have a better idea?" I asked.

"Yes," he whispered. "Texas."

"There is a lot of hostile territory between here and Texas," I said quietly. "We'd have to cut across southwest Missouri to the Texas Road, and the Federals have that territory all bottled up. But Kentucky is ripe for picking, and when the time comes we could make a dash for Virginia and surrender with the regular army."

"No surrender for me," Jim Little declared.

"Better than swinging at the end of a rope," I said.

The cook's helper, a boy of fifteen with reassuringly clean hands, came in with a steaming platter of food—bacon, eggs, biscuits. I swept the map from the table to make room. The boy set the platter carefully on the table, then began to retrieve some plates from the sideboard.

"Smells good," I said.

"I hope you choke on it," Applewaith muttered.

Unfortunately, the whiskey glow had worn off and Applewaith's sniping had become truly annoying. I asked Jim Little to explain things. He sprang up so quickly that he knocked his chair over. Then he drew his Navy pistol, pried the captain's jaw open with his free hand, and thrust the octagonal barrel into his mouth. The brass bead on the top of the barrel that served as a front sight chipped one of Applewaith's front teeth.

"Let me explain how this works," Jim Little said sternly. "We're going to sit down and enjoy our breakfast. You're going to keep your filthy mouth shut. And should any of us so much as get the piles from eating this food, we're going to ride back here and I'm going to do this"— here he thumbed the hammer back—"and send a ball through the back of your neck."

"Jimmie," I said. "That would ruin the chair. Come eat your breakfast."

Jim Little withdrew his pistol, lowered the hammer, and thrust the piece back into his belt. But his dark eyes were still burning as the boy placed a shining plate in front of him. He started to spoon eggs onto the plate, but soon threw down his fork in disgust.

"I can't eat with the smell of Yankee piss in here," he said.

I called for Glasscock. When he stuck his bald head in the doorway, I told him to take the Yankee officers and place them with their men. A moment after Glasscock had dragged them from the room, Frank James and his little brother Dingus walked into the dining room. James was twenty-one, tall and thin, and had been in more scraps—both with the regular army and with partisans—than any of the other boys. He probably also had the best education, and to relax he would retrieve a volume of Shakespeare from his saddlebags while the other boys whored or smoke and drank.

His brother was seventeen, and not been in the war long; he had mostly served with Anderson, and at Centralia he had proved himself capable of killing Yankees of assorted rate and rank, but he was also a bit clumsy. His given name was Jesse, but after he clipped the end of his finger off while loading his revolver, he was universally referred to as Dingus.

"Captain," James said, touching a forefinger to his hat.

Then he slung a flour sack onto the table. The sack landed heavily on the oak top and the cloth split, hemorrhaging gold and silver coins across the table.

"That's the contents of the hotel cash box and what we could find in the house on the hill," James said. "The Yankee captain had a month's pay hidden beneath a loose floorboard in the bedroom."

"One would think they would abandon that practice, seeing as how the floorboards are always the first place we check," I said. "Did you count it?"

"Close to a thousand dollars, mostly in silver," he said.

Jim Little handed me a worn valise, and with a motion of my forearm I scooped most of the coins into it. But I left a pile of coins about the size of a man's fist, and I pushed these over to Frank.

"Obliged," Frank said, scooping the coins into his coat pocket. His little brother said nothing, but his blue eyes shone brightly.

"Captain," Frank said, "may I ask a question?"

I told him he could.

"What is our objective?"

"My objective is to have breakfast," I said.

"It is a serious question, Bill," Frank said. "The men look up to you. We know it's long past time we could make a difference in this war, and the best we can hope is to negotiate an honorable surrender. But until that opportunity presents itself, what's the plan?"

"I'm still considering the options," I said.

"Bill," Frank said, "you know I'm with you to the end. All I ask is that you don't sell our lives too cheaply to the Yankees."

"Never," I said. "But don't count on dying any time soon, Frank, as Providence may have a few surprises in store for us yet."

Frank left the room with his little brother in tow.

I turned back to my breakfast, but Glasscock popped in again.

"You've got visitors," he said. "Are you receiving?"

"Always," I said, pressing a napkin to my mouth.

A pair of girls walked cautiously into the dining room. They were sisters, of possibly sixteen and eighteen, and both had skin that was the purest white and dark hair that clung in ringlets to their foreheads. The older one clutched a book. The younger one carried a silk pillow with both hands, and on the pillow was a card.

I stood.

"To whom do I have the honor?" I asked.

"I am Violet Gregory and this is my sister, Ivy," the older sister said in a fine, high voice. "We take it upon ourselves to welcome you to Tuscumbia, because we feel it would be the desire of our father, Major Gregory, who is away fighting with General Jo Shelby. We commend you for your service to the glorious cause and welcome you on behalf of the town's true patriots."

Violet nodded to her sister, who stepped forward and knelt before me, the silk pillow extended. On the pillow was a sky-colored ribbon, and I took the ribbon and bid the younger girl to rise.

On the ribbon in a childish script was the legend *To Captain Quantrell with deepest appreciation on the occasion of his libation of Tuscumbia from the Yankee aggressor.* Of course, they misspelled my name and had also missed *liberation* by a couple of letters.

"Thank you," I said, and bowed. "I shall keep the ribbon, like my regard for you both, close to my heart."

Then I kissed their hands in turn.

The girls blushed.

"Thank you," I said.

"Would you mind?" Violet asked, offering the book. It was an autograph album, about half full of signatures of local celebrities I had never heard of. She had a pencil, but I had Jim Little fetch a pen and inkwell from the hotel desk, and I turned the book around and upside down so that what had been the last blank page was now the first. I wrote:

> My horse is at the door,
> And the enemy I soon may see
> But before I go Miss Violet
> Here's a double health to thee.

Here's a sigh to those who love me
And a smile to those who hate
And whatever sky's above me
Here's a heart for every fate.

Though the cannons roar around me
Yet it shall still bear me on
Though dark clouds are above me
It hath springs which may be won.

In this verse as with the wine
The libation I would pour
Should be peace with thine and mine
And a health to thee and all in door.

If you're going to steal, as my father always said, you might as well steal big.

I signed the piece, *Very respectfully, your friend, W.C.Q.* Then I handed the autograph album back, and bent low to receive kisses on both cheeks.

Their smell—that mixture of lavender and vanilla that accompanies freshly scrubbed feminine skin, with a bit of animal scent beneath—made me wish for more time. When one enjoys power, I had found, others will gladly yield what they would have otherwise fought dearly to hold.

"And how did you learn of my presence here?" I asked.

"Oh, Captain, the whole town knows," Violet said. "We feared you might think it rude if you weren't formally welcomed."

"Thank you," I said. "Now, if you'll pardon me."

After they left, Jim Little shot me a worried look.

"If those girls had enough time to make you ribbons

and bows," he said, "then that sergeant who went looking for the canned pears this morning has spread the news halfway to Jefferson City by now."

"The rain will slow them down," I said.

"It slows us as well," Jim Little said.

I sighed.

"You're right," I said. "But as long as we cross the river by dark, we should be all right. Besides, we're dealing with the regular army. They will have to conduct three or four staff meetings to decide how best to pursue us, it will take them time to get the troops ready to march, and then they will discover they don't have rain gear and that will hold them up a few more hours, and of course all the delays will secretly please the officers because they don't really want to catch us anyway."

Jim Little stabbed a slab of ham with his knife and flipped it onto his plate.

"The regular army doesn't worry me," I said. "The local militia is of no concern. What does worry me is that sooner or later, they'll think of hiring somebody who is just like us to catch us."

Jim Little laughed.

"Then what are you worried about?" he asked. "There ain't nobody like us."

A Thousand Less One

That afternoon, the rain slacked and the boys were taken across the Osage River in groups of six or eight in a rope-drawn ferry while Jim Little and I watched from the landing. On the first trip, the guns and ammunition that had been taken from the hotel armory and placed in the bed of the wagon were dumped in the middle of the river.

An hour before, I had paroled the prisoners.

"Do you promise," I asked, "to return to your homes and never again take up arms against the Confederate State of America or to speak ill of myself or this company for so long as you all shall live, so help you God?"

"What happens if we don't?" Hensley had asked.

"We shoot you, of course," Jim Little had replied.

All agreed to the terms of the parole, even though I was sure none of them would live by it. Applewaith, of course, berated Hensley for accepting the terms of the parole, but agreed to behave himself until we were on the far side of the Osage.

When the ferry returned for the last trip, Jim Little turned to me and asked who I wanted to set fire to the hotel and the house on the hill. Frank James was still on our side of the river, as was Dick Glasscock, who had found a crate of incendiary grenades in the hotel armory.

"It would be a good chance to see what they can do," Jim Little suggested.

"How many buildings do you suppose we've put to the torch in the last four years?" I asked. "How many homes, how many businesses? Counting sheds and barns and outbuildings."

"Bill, I don't know," he said. "What difference does it make?"

"Several hundred," I said. "Close to a thousand, perhaps."

"Then let's make it an even thousand," Jim Little said.

"It's winter," I said. "And a bad one."

"The Yankees are using the hotel as a barracks, Bill," Jim Little said.

"The rain will put out the fire," I said. "It's just a sprinkle now, but look at that sky. It will pour again, and soon. No, Jim Little, we will cross the Osage and leave no fires behind. We took the garrison and pulled its teeth without firing a shot. Let that be the last word on the Tuscumbia raid."

On the other side of the river after the last crossing, we sank the ferry.

Oliver Shepherd and Dick Glasscock took axes and caved in the side, and as the river poured in, they cut the lines and let it drift with the current until it finally slipped out of sight beneath the mud-colored water.

"Guess that is that," the Yankee boy Jackson said. He was a freckled seventeen-year-old. His hands were tied behind his back, so he was having a little trouble keeping his balance in the saddle.

"Free his hands," I told Dick Glasscock. "He's going to fall from the saddle and dash his brains out on a rock."

Glasscock produced his great knife. He leaned over in his saddle and, in one swipe, severed the boy's bonds.

Jackson seemed a bit surprised that both of his hands were still attached.

"How did somebody with the name Thomas Jefferson Jackson end up as a private in the Federal militia?" I asked.

"My grandfather was a member of the Corps of Discover and later fought at the Battle of New Orleans," the boy said, flinging the ends of rope away and rubbing his wrists. "He was a legend in my family, a backwoods patriarch on the order of Abraham. I am something less."

I laughed.

"Are you going to kill me when I'm no longer of use?" the boy asked.

"Are you going to lead us true?" I asked.

"I will," he said.

"Then your life will be your own after a day or so," I said.

"I can lead you east as far as Maries County," he said.

"We are going south," I said. "How well do you know that terrain?"

"I know it a little," he said. "It is pleasant country, and while hunting I have followed the river bottoms as far as Camden County. Beyond that, the hills become steeper and eventually the land becomes a wilderness that is known by few."

Two days later Jackson and I were riding ahead of the column and had stopped on a small hill overlooking a creek. It was three o'clock in the afternoon but already the shadows were long upon the ground, as it was getting close to the shortest day of the year.

Jackson stood in the stirrups and shaded his eyes from the glare of the low sun.

"Follow the creek until it turns to the east, about two miles below, and there you will find a rocky ford," he said. "Leave the creek and follow the trace to the south. Beyond that, I cannot be of service."

I nodded.

"What will you report to Applewaith upon your return?"

"That I loosened my bonds and escaped in the middle of the night while you and your band were sleeping off a truly legendary drunk," he said. "Then I will draft them an elaborate map which shows you on a bearing for St. Louis. That'll throw them into a five-alarm panic."

I laughed. "You have no compunction about lying?"

"Your reputation is bad, but I wasn't in Lawrence or any of those other places they talk about," he said. "You've treated me well and left Tuscumbia standing, so that's what I have to go on. Besides, if I told the truth and did my duty, that would force a confrontation and men would die. I would rather not be responsible for that."

"You're a good lad," I said, "but a poor soldier."

"How you flatter me," Jackson said. "I have had enough of army life; it seems an exercise in the abuse of power and the glorification of stupidity, and a colossal waste of human material. It is organized tragedy, for no apparent purpose, and the prospect of glory is an empty promise. The smallpox has taken far more of our company than bullets ever could, and I can think of no death more ignoble."

Then his attention was distracted by something on the other side of the creek. I turned to look, and by the time I saw the glint of gunmetal a half mile away, a cloud of white smoke was blossoming in the same place.

Then I turned back to warn Jackson, but it was too late—a dark hole had appeared in his forehead, and a spray of pink mist had bloomed behind his head. The sound of the gunshot came as Jackson was falling dead from the saddle.

Jim Little and Frank James crested the hill at the head of the column as the second shot came. I heard the ball whistle past my ear.

"Sniper," I said.

Instead of wheeling their horses and taking cover, they drove forward and led the column down the hill and splashing across the creek. There were a couple of shots from the timber, but the column did not slow, and as they entered the trees, the popping of revolvers came as quickly as fireworks on the Fourth of July.

When they returned, Frank James was cradling a Whitworth rifle with a telescopic tube sight. The rifles were British, took a hex-shaped bullet, and were slow to load—but deadly at ranges of nearly a mile.

"Here's a prize," he said.

He tossed me the rifle, which I caught in my left hand. The rifle's stock was splattered with blood and bits of bone and hair.

"How many were there?" I asked.

"Two," he said. "They were on foot. Deserters, from the looks of it."

"Shooting at their own men?"

"Rebel deserters," Frank said. "But I don't think it would have made any difference. Before I blew the brains out of the back of his head, the sharpshooter said he just saw a couple of men on horseback and wanted the horses. And it was a good thing he was a bad shot."

"He drilled Jackson right in the forehead."

"Yeah, but he said he was aiming at you."

"I don't want this," I said, holding out the Whitworth. "They're slow to load, they're heavy, and you can never find the special hex-shaped bullets they require. Besides, it is a weapon that is ill-suited to my temperament—it is an assassin's weapon, and one which relieves you of the weight of seeing the expression on your enemy's face. It makes me sick."

I slung the Whitworth back to Frank.

"Throw it in the creek," I said.

Then I turned to Jim Little.

"Bury Jackson here on the hillside," I said. "Mark the grave with a cairn of stones so that they may recover the body when the war is over. But leave the deserters to rot."

A Passing of Shadows

The rivers froze and the ground turned to iron, and in a fortnight we found ourselves in the wilderness, as Jackson had promised. We picked up the ice-clabbered Eleven Point River and followed the eastern bank through a silent winter landscape.

The weather continued to worsen, and although we were well provisioned from our raid at Tuscumbia, the cold began to take its toll. Bivouacs were becoming difficult, because of the lack of population and the consequent scarcity of barns and outbuildings in which to take shelter for a few hours of sleep; we traveled light, and although we had bedrolls, we never had tents or any other type of camp equipment. More often than not, any sleep we got was in the saddle. Then one afternoon it began to snow, large flakes that fell like leaves from a leaden sky, and when Jim Little nudged me and pointed to chimney smoke on the horizon, I nodded gratefully.

Carrying in the still air was the distant baying of hounds.

We turned the column to the east and made our way through a mile or so of dead buffalo grass that was be-

coming heavy with snow and ground broken by many
creeks and ravines. Then we entered a heavily wooded
area and picked our way down a trace and finally
emerged in a meadow, where there was a cluster of several one-room cabins. In a clearing not far from the cabins was a church of plank and hewn logs, and atop the
rough steeple was an unpainted wooden cross.

The smoke was coming from the rough stone chimney
of the cabin nearest the church. I ordered the boys to hold
in the trees while Jim Little and I rode forward to inves-
tigate.

The cabins had an unoccupied look about them; even
with the crust of snow over everything, it was apparent
that weeds and brambles had encroached right up to their
wooden steps, and there were no animals in the pens out
back. A few of the cabins had been partially burned, and
their gaping roofs allowed the snow to fall right in. And
even though it was late enough in the afternoon that the
snow had taken on a decidedly blue cast, not a hint of
warm yellow shone behind the canvas that covered any of
the windows.

"Hallo," Jim Little said as we approached the cabin
with the chimney smoke. "Hallo the cabin. Anybody
home?"

There was no response.

"At least they didn't shoot," I said.

"Not yet, anyway," Jim said, sliding down from the
saddle to the ground.

While he walked through the snow, up the steps, and
onto the porch, I drew my Army in case there was trouble. Jim Little hollered again, then stamped back and
forth on the porch, to make sure his presence was
known.

"All right," he said. "You know we're here."

Then he drew his revolver and kicked open the door. He ducked to the side, anticipating a shot, but it wasn't necessary. The plank door hung by one leather hinge, at a skewed angle, revealing the interior.

The cabin was empty.

I dismounted and dropped the reins in the snow, knowing Old Charley would stay right where he was until I returned. Joining Jim Little in the cabin, we discovered a well-banked fire in the hearth, but no sign of the owner. There was a rough plank table beneath the window on the east side of the cabin, and a rough rope bed on the other side, and a three-legged stool near the fireplace. There were a few signs of habitation—a pot, a cup, and a plate, a filthy blanket piled on the bed—but not much else.

Jim Little returned his revolver to his belt, then nodded to a crucifix hanging on the wall over the bed. "They may not have much, but at least they're thankful," he said.

"And literate," I said.

There was a book on the table, a Douay Bible, and I walked over and glanced at the open pages.

"The time of our life is short and tedious, and in the end of a man there is no remedy, and no man hath been known to have returned from hell," I read aloud. "For we are born of nothing, and after this we shall be as if we had not been, for the breath in our nostrils is smoke, and speech a spark to move our heart, which being put out, our body shall be ashes . . . And our name in time shall be forgotten, and no man shall have any remembrance of our works, for our time is the passing of a shadow."

"That's cheerful," Jim Little said. "I don't remember ever hearing that in Sunday school. What the hell kind of Bible are you reading from?"

"Catholic," I said. "It's from Wisdom, a book not found in the Protestant Bible."

"Papists, huh?" Jim Little asked suspiciously.

"It would seem," I said.

Like most of the boys, Jim Little had about as much firsthand knowledge of Catholics as he did the Musselmans, but he was sure that they were up to no good; because of a couple of lurid and questionable accounts published in Boston about thirty years ago, just about everybody knew that nunneries were nothing more than brothels for the priests, that the basements were filled with the bodies of newborn babes killed to keep the secret, and that the pope himself was competing with the Jews in a vast conspiracy to corrupt and then dominate the civilized world.

You've heard of this, no?

Well, just when those half-baked anti-Catholic ideas were about to expire on their own, they were revived by the furor over Irish immigration. People got so worked up over the issue that they wanted to send immigrants back to their home country, deny them employment, make *Protestant* Bible readings mandatory for their children, and increase the waiting period for citizenship to twenty-one years.

That's right, a generation.

Things came to a head when the pope sent a stone to be included in the Washington Monument, and the Native American Party—better known as the Know Nothings—stole the stone in 1854 and threw it into the Potomac River. Then they took over the building committee, on the grounds that the monument wasn't American enough with all of those foreign stones being donated, and since then have mucked up the works so badly by arguing over what constitutes true patriotism that any real work on the obelisk has since stopped.

Jim Little, of course, had all of these foolish ideas swirling around in his brain. He also could have served as a model for the party mascot, "Citizen Know Nothing— Uncle Sam's Youngest Son"—he had the fair skin, the wavy hair, and the perfectly oblong brain pan preferred by strict nativists.

"Fix the door and then tell the men to bed down in whatever cabins still have a roof over them," I said. "Catholic or no, this is a good place to hole up until the storm blows over."

I started for the door.

"Where are you going?" Jim Little asked.

"To the church to look for our host," I said.

Old Charley, having a nearly white coat, was all but invisible against the field of snow. I reached down and grasped his reins and pulled him behind me as I crossed the fifty yards to the church. There was a lonely little graveyard out back, defined by a split-rail fence, where a few wooden grave markers stood above the snow. In the west, the setting sun was a glowing red ball framed by the black branches of the bare trees. My shadow on the snow was a tall specter leading a ghostly horse. The snow crunched beneath my boots. The cold scalded my throat and lungs and as I watched my breath hang in the still air, I thought of the verse I had read aloud in the cabin.

Our breath truly is smoke, I thought, *and our time is the passing of a shadow.*

A shiver ran down my spine, and I told myself to stop engaging in such foolishness. I trudged around to the front of the church, which faced to the east. The double wooden doors were opened a crack, and a narrow shaft of candlelight was thrown upon the snow. I left Old Charley in the snow, mounted the wooden steps, and pushed one of the doors open with my hand.

I started to call out for the priest, but the scene that presented itself as the door swung open caused the breath to seize in my throat. There was a single lighted candle on the altar, and on a bench placed on the footpace below was the body of a young woman. She was nude, and her torso was draped in white samite, the folds of which fluttered in the winter gust I had admitted by the opening of the door; the candle flame also flared and threatened to gutter, making the scene dance and quiver before my disbelieving eyes.

I stood for a moment on the threshold, undecided, thinking it better perhaps to leave but at the same time unable to deny my fascination. So I stepped inside and gently shut the door behind me.

"Forgive me," I said loudly. "Is anyone here?"

There was no answer.

I removed my gloves and tucked them in my belt. Then I walked down the aisle, touching the backs of the rough pews with the palm of my right hand. I passed through the gate in the communion rail and entered the sanctuary.

While the church was simplicity itself, with walls of plank and a floor of puncheon, the sanctuary was a marvel of carpentry in native wood. In the canopy Christ hung upon His cross, and beneath Him was the tabernacle covered in a veil of green, and radiating from this was the rest of the stair-stepped and ornate altar in walnut and pecan and oak and ash and others I cannot name.

As I mounted the altar steps and neared the body, I recognized her funeral drape as merely rough cotton and not the glittering cloth of myth. My eyes had been tricked by light and shadow.

The woman had been tall, and her body did not quite fit the bench on which she had been placed. Her head was tilted back and her thick red hair fell in ringlets to the floor. At the opposite end of the bench, her small feet jutted at an awkward angle. Her hands were clasped beneath her breasts. Her hands were finely shaped and her fingers were slender, but her fingernails were cracked and chipped. Her features were superior—she had a smooth forehead and cheeks, a fine nose, and her lips, though bluish, were well formed.

A wooden bucket was beside the bench upon which her body lay, and a soiled rag was beside it. I touched the bucket with the toe of my boot, and found that the wine-colored water had frozen to ice.

I looked more closely at the body, trying to determine the source of the blood in the bucket, but could find none. Carefully, I lifted the cloth and found a dark spot about the size of the tip of my little finger high upon her left breast. The muzzle of the gun must have been within inches, for around the wound, her porcelain skin was peppered with gunpowder.

Then I replaced the cloth and touched my hand to her face. Her body was frozen just as solid as the water in the bucket and her cheek was so cold that it seemed to burn against my palm. I withdrew my hand, but fought an irrational urge to bow down and kiss those marbled lips, in an attempt to restore a little warmth to the broken vessel.

"Who killed you?" I whispered.

It was a felo-de-se.

I cannot describe how cruelly the realization struck me—it weakened my knees as would a killing blow, and

I sank to the floor beside the bier. To think that this beautiful creature had been so taken with despair to take her own life, and in so doing had consigned her soul to an eternity in hell, was too much for me to bear.

"Oh God, no!" I cried out.

Then a hand in black grasped my shoulder.

I whirled and produced my Army.

Staring down at me was a grizzled old man.

He was small, like a child, and his hair shockingly white and his eyes milky. In one hand he held the haft of a shovel that was thrown over his shoulder and the other hand, in a black glove, was raised in a fist against me. When he spoke, I knew he had been born in Ireland.

"Go ahead and shoot, you bleeding fool," he challenged.

"Who are you?"

"Shoot, and you'll never find out," he grumbled. "Then you'll have both me and the girl to bury, and with the ground so hard even Samson himself couldn't dig a grave. But it would be a blessing, because being murdered is an easier way to paradise than dying of starvation. Have you any food?"

"The cemetery is out back," I said. "You weren't there when I came in."

"She ain't going in consecrated ground, you idiot," the old man said, turning away from me and letting the shovel clang to the floor. "She's a suicide, a self-murderer, not fit to bury with Christ's children. No food, eh?"

"Why, in God's name, is she nude?"

"Had to wash the body," he said. "Oh, don't give me that look. I'm so damned old and so bleeding hungry that a ham sandwich looks better to me than a pretty girl. She's a suicide, and must be buried without a stitch, with no coffin, at a crossroads. It's ordained."

"I've never heard of that tradition," I said. "You weren't going to . . . you weren't going to butcher her for dinner, were you?"

"Aw, you're daft," the old man said with a dismissive wave. "If I didn't eat my neighbors during the potato famine, when I had all my teeth, do you think I'd turn to cannibalism now?"

"Well, the Donner Party . . ."

"You're just like all the rest in this country, you have no memory for what's gone before but you believe yourself an expert on every damned thing under the sun. Tell me, are you a Rebel or a Unionist? Oh hell, never mind, I don't care. One is just as bad as the other."

"Who are you?" I asked again.

"Call me Paddy, you all do," the old man said. "Dammit, man, have you any victuals or not?"

"Yes, I will feed you presently," I said. "But I require answers. Where is everybody? Where's the priest?"

"Gone, dead, starved or robbed or burned out by the raiders," he said. "We declared ourselves neutral at the start of the war. That just made us targets for both sides. Father Hogan left three years ago—I suppose he's back in St. Louis by now, the priests usually make out all right, makes me wish for the old days when the Vikings spared not the clergy."

"So you're from St. Louis?"

"May the ghost of Mary Malone and her nine bastard children chase you so far over the hills of damnation that the Good Lord Himself can't find you with a telescope," the old man sighed. "Of course I'm from St. Louis. That's what I bleeding said, wasn't it?"

"Stop cursing," I said. "Please."

"No," he said, prefacing the negative with an old and particularly obscene word.

"What was her name?"

"Elaine Corbin," he said. "She was seventeen."

"Were you related?"

"Do we bloody look like we're related?" he asked. "I've known her since she was a little girl in Dogtown. Her family moved back to the slums of St. Louis in the winter of 1863, after the bastards in blue burned their cabin. They were one of the last families to go back, back to where we should have been—we were the city poor, and no amount of hoeing could turn us into country folk. Hell, we even lived like we still did in the city, with all the cabins crowded here together in a little neighborhood. Wilderness—to the devil with it. If I wasn't so damned old, I'd walk all the way back to Dogtown myself."

"But what about Elaine Corbin?"

"She was in love with the oldest Donnelly boy and she cried so to break your heart when he went back with his family to Dogtown. They promised each other that, on her seventeenth birthday, they would meet here at the church and never again part."

"And she took her life because he betrayed her," I concluded.

"No," the old man said. "She took her life because the promise was kept."

"You speak in riddles," I said.

"Look at the grave markers in the cemetery out back," he said, "and you will find the name of David Donnelly, who was killed during a raid last August. His family moved on west. They wrote to her, but the letter never found her."

"And she blamed herself for his death."

"I don't know," he said. "I returned from hunting two days ago and found Elaine Corbin dead atop David Donnelly's grave, an old single-shot pistol in her hand and a ball through her breast. She had been dead some time, and left no note—but then, she didn't need to. And, she kept her promise, didn't she? You have to admire that kind of sand."

The door burst open and Jim Little strode inside, a revolver in each hand.

"You need some help, Bill?"

"Lord, not another one," the old man said.

"You'd been gone for such a spell that I—" He stopped when he saw the dead girl on the bench. "I see what has commanded your attention. Is this a private Papist ceremony, or can anybody join?"

"Put your guns away," I said. "The girl needs burial."

"I can see that," he said.

"Didn't hear a shot," Jim Little said.

"I didn't kill her," I said.

"Did you undress her?"

"Jimmie, this is how I found her."

"I'll fetch a blanket," Jim Little said, turning away.

"Of course," I said, ashamed that a blanket hadn't been my first impulse.

Then I told Jim Little to bring back four or five of the boys to start a fire.

"A fire?" Jim Little asked. "You going to torch the church?"

It wasn't such a bad idea—it would have suited a range of sensibilities, from Viking to Hindu—but I didn't think it was what Elaine Corbin would have wanted.

"No, we're going to use the fire to thaw the ground so that we can dig a grave in the morning," I said. "Take one of the wrecked cabins apart for fuel."

"A fire like that, burning all night," Jim Little said. "It's a beacon. Could attract Yankees."

"Not so long as it keeps snowing," I said.

Jim Little nodded and left the church.

Far off, a pack of hounds began to howl, signaling a chase.

"Ah," the old man said. "My dogs. They nearly have their supper. Now, where's mine?"

A Chipped Tooth

Elaine Corbin came to me that night.

She rose from the bier and walked down the aisle of the dark church and stepped barefoot into the snow outside. In her passage she lost her shroud and when she appeared at the door of the cabin in which Jim Little and I slept, she was nude. It was still snowing and the flakes swirled and skittered across the floor and I knew she was there, standing in the open doorway, even though my face was to the ceiling.

I tried to turn my head, but found I could not.

Of course, at this point you will say I was dreaming. Let me tell you directly that it was no dream; I was tired, but not asleep, and when the cabin door opened, I heard it clearly and felt the cold blast of air it admitted. But I could not move. And when I attempted to call out to wake Jim Little, I found that I had been rendered mute.

A terror crept over me that I had not known since childhood.

As a man, I discovered that nothing on earth was to be feared. A man—or woman—with a revolver was the equal of any other and, depending upon skill, perhaps even better; the worst that another could do to me, through skill or luck or treachery, was to kill me. Why, there is nothing to be feared in that—everybody dies sooner or later; it's as easy as falling off a log, and I'd witnessed enough of the actual thing to know that fear of it was much worse than the actual thing. The fear of death is the most perverted kind of abstraction. No matter how hard they fight it in the minutes or hours or days before, at the actual moment they slip quietly beneath the waters of death and their countenance becomes serene, even beatific.

No, I do not fear death—it is the *prospect* of fear that I despise, and the creeping cancer of despair. When I was a child, I was afraid of the dark, and I was afraid of the dark because, just at that moment when one is about to drift off to sleep, I would find myself seized by an inexplicable paralysis. Although I could swivel my eyes, I could move not a finger, and often I would feel a terrible weight upon my chest.

And the weight was unspeakably demonic.

The fear of these episodes turned my nights into sweating, shaking, nail-biting ordeals. I dared not sleep at night. When I could light a candle without being discovered, I would read to keep myself awake—novels, mostly, starting with Walter Scott's *Ivanhoe*, but also newspapers and the illustrated weeklies. I would force myself to read until the sky began to lighten in the east, and then—and only then—would I lay aside the book and sleep until being roughly thrown from bed by my mother.

She was wholly without maternal instincts. That was owing, perhaps, to her having been orphaned by an epidemic at an early age and taken in by a cruel family named Clarke. She spoke little of her childhood, but I gathered it must have been horrid. She no longer had contact with the Clarke family, and it is no wonder, for I never heard her say a kind word about them.

Still, that was no reason to make mine miserable. On the contrary, one would think that a mother with an unhappy childhood would want something better for her children, but with Caroline Clarke Quantrill, that was not the case. The more her children suffered, the more it seemed to ease her own memories.

When I attempted to relate my own nightly ordeals, she would hear none of it. She would fly into a rage, accuse me of being lazy and a fabulist, and once she became so inflamed that she struck me across the mouth, and I fell and chipped one of my front teeth on the gridiron of the fireplace.

Mother pleaded with me not to tell my father, and suggested instead a fabrication—one of many—in which I tripped over my own shoes, which I had carelessly left in the middle of the floor.

My father had a penchant for beating me over any real or perceived shortcoming, and I was not anxious to bring another barrage by confessing my night terrors.

You might think my father was an uneducated man, but just the opposite is true; he was a literate man, a schoolteacher and an author of sorts, having written a treatise on tinsmithing. There was some unpleasantness over the tinsmith book because he had borrowed money without permission from the school fund for its printing, convinced that he would quickly make his fortune and be able to replace the funds without harm, but a disagreeable man named Beeson discovered and misunderstood the arrangement. My father was so incensed at having his reputation maligned that he determined to kill Beeson, and arrived at the home with a derringer in order to do just that; but, by luck, Beeson was heating a cup of cider with a hot poker, and he brought the poker down on my father's head before the just bullet could be delivered. My father's cracked skull recovered, as did his reputation, for he was eventually made master of the Canal Dover School.

My father was a collector of books, so I had an ample library to choose from, and I absorbed knowledge as if by osmosis—without meaning to, I had given myself an education, just at the time when a child absorbs information like a sponge. And while these night watches fed my mind, they turned my days into bleary, sleepwalking affairs. In turn, the fear and anxiety of these attacks of paralysis and lack of sleep fostered a deep despair, and when I was ten or twelve years of age the world grew dim and silent, lacking not only mirth but even hope.

Although my family was not of the churchgoing persuasion, my reading eventually made me curious about religion and I began to feverishly seek comfort in the Bible, by the glow of a midnight taper. And even though I read both the Old and New Testaments from cover to cover, several times, I found nothing in it that would ward off the near-sleep illness.

Eventually I grew out of both the night terrors and the nocturnal Bible study. When, at the age of fifteen or sixteen, I discovered some innate ability with the caplock pistol, I began to sleep soundly. It was about the time that my father died of consumption. I was also big enough by then that my mother could not easily chip another tooth, and when she discovered my ability with shooting arms, she began to treat me with a certain deference.

But the old fear returned that night in the cabin in the wilderness.

With the corpse of Elaine Corbin at the door—I was again afraid of the dark, I was afraid of despair, I was afraid of death. Worst of all, I again found myself in the grip of an inexplicable paralysis.

Desperately, I wished for a Bible.

I heard her bare feet cross the floor, felt her weight upon the pallet where I slept, and my nostrils were filled with the sweet odor of slowly rotting flesh. My mouth was silent, but my mind was screaming. Why, I thought piteously to myself, had the ghost of the beautiful suicide sought me out?

Just as the terrible dark shadow loomed over me and I knew I could stand it no more, the cabin was shot with a brilliant light. I cannot identify the source of the light, which was light, but was more than light. It blazed as white as the sun and revealed, to my astonishment, that Elaine Corbin was not a rotting corpse come to drag my soul to hell, but a beautiful apparition that floated above me. Her hair was like a halo around her and she regarded me with the kind of love a mother might have for a child.

"Be not afraid," she said, her green eyes shining. "Thrice we shall meet. By grace I bring you this warning—turn not away. By faith I bring you this promise—turn not away. By love I bring you this counsel—turn not away."

Then her lips met mine, and I found they were warm and sweet.

The snow stopped just after dawn and Glasscock and Hockensmith and a few of the others found shovels and axes and began to work on the ground above the grave of David Donnelly. There was nobody to argue with about the location of the grave, because the old man was gone; his absence was discovered about the same time that one of the horses was found to be missing, and I assumed he was headed back to his beloved St. Louis slum.

The fire was just embers now, but it had done its work

in softening the frozen crust, and within an hour the boys had the grave excavated down to the lid of the coffin. Then Frank James attempted to climb out of the grave, and Glasscock put a hand down to pull him up, but he slipped and his boot came heavily down on top of the coffin, splintering the rotten wood and crushing the rib cage of the skeleton beneath.

I was annoyed.

Sternly I had instructed them not to disturb the remains of the Donnelly boy, and of course that very thing had happened. Frank's little brother, Dingus, took a few steps back from the grave, but Glasscock threw his bald head back and laughed, showing those rows of cannibal teeth.

"Dammit," Frank muttered, trying to withdraw his boot. He managed to get it out of the coffin, but he took most of the lid with it, revealing the skull with a gaping jaw.

Frank paused, then reached down into the grave, and plucked up the skull by its eye sockets. Then he tucked the skull beneath his arm and, clasping Glasscock's offered hand in his own, pulled himself up onto the fresh mound of dirt.

"Put it back, Frank," Dingus said.

But Frank struck a dramatic pose, rested one hand on the butt of his revolver, and held the skull at arm's length.

"Faith, not a jot, but to follow him thither with modesty enough," Frank recited imperfectly. "Alexander died, Alexander was buried, Alexander returneth to dust; the dust is earth, of earth we make loam, and of that loam, was converted. Imperious Caesar, dead and turned to clay, might stop a hole to keep the wind away. Oh, that that earth, which kept the world in awe, should patch a wall to expel the winter flaw!"

Frank drew the skull to his cheek, then turned the skull as if it were casting a sly look at me.

"Here comes the king!" Frank said.

Glasscock howled.

"You make a poor Hamlet," I said. "And unlike Yorick, I am not a man of infinite jest."

I should have been more stern, but then I remembered how Byron drank wine from the skullcap of a long-dead monk and declared it to be a more practical use than to which most heads are employed.

Jim Little, however, took the matter personally.

"Stop that desecration," he said.

"I'm with him," Dingus said. "Stop it, Frank."

"Memento mori," Frank said. *"Nunc est bibendum, nunc pede libero pulsanda tellus."*

"It is rude to speak a foreign tongue among those who don't understand it," Jim Little groused.

"Not just a foreign tongue, but a dead one," Frank said. "But the captain understands it. You've had a smattering of Latin, haven't you, Bill?"

"I remember that I am mortal, Frank," I said. "And now may be the only time I have to drink and to dance footloose upon the earth, but I choose not. There is more important business to attend to."

"With that attitude," Frank said, "you'll never get around to drinking or dancing. But take a good look, boys, because this is where we're all bound, sooner or later—and, the way things are going, I'd say sooner."

"It ain't funny," Dingus said.

"Wasn't meant to be, Jesse."

"Sometimes," Dingus said, "I think you're the smartest dumb person I ever met."

For brothers, they seemed an odd pair, as if they had been raised in different countries. There was four or five years between them, but it wasn't just their ages that made them seem strangers to one another—Frank was well read, even-tempered, and a cool fighter, while Dingus was a dreamy and spoiled child and seemed only to pay attention when angry. Frank had been with me from the start, but Dingus had been with Anderson only for a year or two and had been with me only since the rendezvous in Fayette County.

"Come out of there and return the skull to its rest," Jim Little said. "Fetch the girl's body and let's be done with this task, because this episode in its entirety has made me unnatural anxious."

I had not told him of the night visitation.

The boys lifted the body of Elaine Corbin, which had been sewn into a Federal blanket, upon their shoulders and solemnly carried it out of the church and to the waiting grave. They gently lowered her down to the embrace of her lover, and then they looked to me to say some words. Everybody was quiet except for Joe Hall, who couldn't stifle his cough.

I glanced over at Frank, and he nodded.

"Lay her in the earth, and from her fair and unpolluted flesh, may violets spring," Frank said. Then he took up a shovel, scooped up some dirt, and heaved it into the grave. "Now pile your dust upon the quick and the dead."

The Snowball Skirmish

We crossed quietly into Arkansas around Christmas, but the view didn't change much: hills and trees and snow. Conversation among us dwindled to nothing, because we had exhausted every subject of any possible interest, so we rode mostly in silence.

Perhaps it was the season that got me to reflecting on home. I wondered what my mother was doing at that moment, how my poor sister Mary with the crooked spine was getting on, how the little brothers were, and whether there was a Christmas tree up in the old home place. Do they have enough to eat? I wondered.

I had not written them since the year before the war, when I was teaching school at Stanton, in Kansas Territory, and even then I was discouraged because I would write three or five letters to them for every one I received. Eventually, I stopped. I had kept up a constant string of epistles to them about every damned thing—Salt Lake City, the expedition to the Kansas gold fields, the near-starvation on the snowy banks of Pikes Peak, the return to Stanton and the little community of men from Dover and the thousand small betrayals—and I attempted to portray a cheerful disposition, but I suppose some cool thoughts came through anyway.

How strange. All of those letters to my mother were written while I was still a Free State man, thought Jim Lane was the finest and wisest gentleman in the West, and regarded all Democrats as rascals and looked forward to the day when they would, like Jews, be scattered by the four winds to the ends of the earth. I had not told my family of my conversion to the Southern cause, although they may have divined it from the newspapers, but I doubt it; for Mother, newspapers were about as much of a mystery as a bicycle would be to a baboon. Reading and writing of any kind, in fact, proved a nearly superhuman chore for her, and when I did get a letter from her, I winced at the misspellings and tortured syntax.

Did I call my mother a baboon?

So be it. There is more than a passing resemblance.

Thinking about my family got me to thinking about my childhood friends, and I wondered for perhaps the thousandth time where William Walter Scott might be. In a Yankee uniform, no doubt, and every time we encountered an Ohio unit I was on the lookout for him. When last I saw him we were both teenagers. Walter worked as a printer's devil at one of the local newspapers, had an inquisitive mind, and was a ready source of mischief.

We would capture field mice during the week in order to release them in church on Sunday, ignite fireworks on the steps of the local constable at midnight, and string tin cans to the tail of a hound and then set him loose upon the thoroughfare at noon on a weekday. Timing, Walter said, was the best part of any prank—

that which is funniest occurs when (and where) it is least expected.

As we grew older, the pranks became more elaborate.

On the last night of March, we spent all night setting type at the *Iron Valley Reporter* for a story that the petrified body of Adam had been found just outside town, and that the six-thousand-year-old corpse lacked the requisite number of ribs and that an apple had been found in his mouth; we hid spoiled meat beneath the floorboards of the schoolhouse on the hottest day of September so that we wouldn't be held a minute more than necessary; and we led younger boys into the woods with gunnysacks and corncob calls for snipe hunts.

Then one midnight toward the end of October we found ourselves in a cemetery and Walter had a shovel and a candle and was trying to talk me into digging up one of the older graves in order to get at the bones. He said he wanted the skull for a jack-o'-lantern. It would be the envy of every other boy in the county, he said, and later we could form our own society and use it in secret and profane rites. But the idea frightened me, so I demurred. Without my help, Walter abandoned his graverobbing plan, but he remained keen on anything that smacked of the macabre.

Not long after, our interests turned from trying to impress the other boys to winning the affections of the fair sex. Being a rascal, Walter of course was very popular with the girls. And while I wasn't exactly unpopular, my confidence was never great enough to engage in any real love affairs; everywhere I turned in old Dover, there seemed to hover the specter of my dead father or the disapproving gaze of my quarrelsome mother.

That changed, of course, when I escaped west.

I remember writing Walter from Kansas Territory

once, and bragging about the girls. "A man can have his choice, for we have all kinds and all colors here," I told him, "black, white, or red, but to tell you which I like the best is a mixture of the latter colors, if properly brought up, for they are both docile and good-looking." When my squaw wife died, I told him, then I would return to Dover for my second wife.

The bastard never wrote me back.

I was riding along thinking about how Walter had never answered my letter and considering the possible reasons—including the possibility that he might have died in the years since I left Dover—when something struck me between the shoulder blades.

At first, I thought I'd been shot dead.

But another white orb sailed past my ear, followed by the sound of raucous laughter, and I realized that I had been struck by a snowball.

"Surrender or prepare to defend yourself!" young Hank Noland called, another white round in his cocked right hand. He was crouched at the side of the road, and I had apparently ridden past him, lost in thought, without seeing. A couple of the other boys, including Dingus James, were kneeling beside him, making fresh ammunition from the material at hand.

I turned Charley and rested my hands on the pommel.

"What terms do you offer?" I asked.

"Terms?" Hank asked. "You are hardly in a position to request terms. Surrender unconditionally or face the consequences."

Jim Little and Frank James had slipped from their saddles and were busy making snowballs.

"Well," I said, "lay on."

Then I slipped from the saddle and Jim Little and Frank and I launched an assault against the younger men, and for a few minutes the snowballs were flying as thick as the cannon shot had at Elkhorn Tavern. The snowballs powdered our chests and thighs and stung our faces, but neither side would give an inch of territory, but instead the volleys became more furious.

"Hey!" Vess Akers said after peppering the center of Frank's chest. "You've gotta go down on that one, that would've scrambled your brains."

"Make me," Frank said, scooping up more ammunition.

Then Dingus let fly with a snowball that had a flat trajectory and it struck Jim Little in the left temple, making a peculiar thudding sound. Jim Little fell to the ground, unconscious, with the rock that had been packed inside the snow beside him.

"Christ on the cross, Jesse," Frank said. "I think you've killed him."

Frank knelt down and began to slap Jim Little's face.

"He deserved it," Dingus said. "He wasn't playing fair. He hit me twice in the face and it stung. And I've got the same kind of round if anybody thinks he didn't have it coming."

"Cease fire," I said, then knelt on the other side of Jim Little.

Blood was running down the side of Jim Little's face, and his eyes were rolled up into the back of his head, making them look like hard-boiled eggs. Frank grabbed a clump of snow and pressed it against the wound, which slowed the bleeding. Then the cold must have brought Jim Little around, for his eyes fluttered and returned to normal, and he sat up.

"I'm going to kill that little sonuvabitch," he said.

He got about halfway up, then lost his balance and fell back into the snow.

"Jesse," Frank said, "make yourself scarce until Jim here has had a chance to cool off. What the hell is wrong with you? That was a damned stupid thing to do, because when you least expect it Jim is going to get satisfaction."

"Aw, that doesn't scare me none," Dingus said.

But he dropped the remaining missile of ice and snow on the ground.

A Black Dog

It was snowing and we were standing about, stamping our feet and blowing into our hands. The sky was the color of dirty laundry. We were in a little valley near the town of Pocahontas in northwest Arkansas, where we had found an old barn. We were waiting for the coffee to boil, and we weren't very talkative and I was thinking about why anybody would name a town in northwestern Arkansas after an Indian princess that lived on the East Coast about three or four centuries ago. Then there was this rumble I felt right through the soles of my boots and it took me a moment to realize that it was thunder.

"I'll be damned," Oliver Shepherd said. "Have you ever heard thunder during a snowstorm?"

"No," I said. "It feels unnatural."

"Is there even a name for it?" Jim Little asked.

"Not that I know of," I said.

Then Isaac Hall came out of the barn toward us.

"Hey, Ike, what's for breakfast?" Glasscock asked.

But Ike ignored the joke. His face was downcast and I knew immediately what was the matter; his little brother, Joseph, lay sick inside the barn, stricken with fever.

"Cap'n, Joe's no better," Ike said.

"I'm sorry to hear that," I said.

"Would you take a look?" he asked.

"I'm not a doctor," I said. "Don't know what I could do."

"Well, you've had more experience than all of us boys put together," he said. "You've been out West, you palavered with the Mormon saints, you were married to an Indian princess, and you survived freezing to death on Pikes Peak. You've seen things . . . I mean, you've seen sickness. Maybe you can tell me if what Joe has looks familiar."

Jim Little and Ol Shepherd fell silent and kept their eyes fastened to the ground. Frank James hooked his thumbs in his belt and shifted his weight from one foot to the other, keeping an eye on his little brother Dingus, who was listening to the conversation with slack-jawed interest.

"All right," I said.

"Obliged," Isaac said.

As I followed him into the rattrap of a barn, Dingus began to follow us, and Frank reached out and clamped a hand around his upper arm.

"Hey," Dingus said. "I just want to take a look. . . ."

"No," Frank said, "you don't. Stay out here."

Joe Hall was off in the far corner of the barn, with his head on his saddle, and blankets piled around him. Even though it was damned cold in the barn, his face was as red as a potbellied stove and shone with sweat.

I knelt, resting my forearms on my knees, and although at least a foot away, I could feel the heat radiating from his body. I called the boy's name.

Joe moaned, his eyelids flickered, and then he muttered something about shucking corn. His hands, which were resting atop the blanket, began to flail.

"He hasn't made any sense for an hour," Ike said, grasping the churning hands. "It's all right, Joe. There's no corn to shuck. It's winter. Just rest, brother."

"Drunk with fever," I said. "When did you first notice him getting sick?"

"He started complaining a couple of days ago about having the shivers. Then he got a headache and started retching over everything," Ike said, uncapping a canteen. He held it to his brother's lips, and Joe drank, then wetted his cracked lips with his tongue.

The tongue was dotted with red sores.

I stood up.

"What's wrong?" Ike asked.

"Let's step back outside," I said.

It had been nearly three weeks since the raid at Tuscumbia, and I was beginning to hope the band had escaped the smallpox. But there was no denying that Joseph Hall had come down hard with it, and would soon spread it to the rest of the men.

The water in the tin can hanging over the fire was boiling now, churning up the coffee grounds with it. Frank James withdrew a kerchief and used it to tip the can to one side, pouring some of the rough coffee into a tin cup. He handed me the cup, and I used a kerchief to keep from burning my hands.

"Joe has smallpox," I said.

Isaac blinked hard, then nodded.

Frank James handed him a cup of coffee.

"Thanks," Ike said, showing a remarkable display of nerve. "I'll stay here and take care of Joe until he dies or recovers well enough to go home. Keep the boys away from him, and away from me, probably."

There was more of that thunder with the snow again.

"Even if you have it, you won't be contagious for a

couple of weeks," I said. "The contagion comes with the sores. Don't let anybody touch Joe's blanket or clothes. Burn them when you're in position to. We'll leave you all the food we can spare, but you'd better hunt when the weather allows."

Jim Little was sitting on a stump a few yards away, listening to all of this with his arms crossed, and he began to shake his head mournfully. I've never seen anybody more superstitious or afraid of sickness than he.

"We're dead," he said, in a kind of chant. "We're all going to die."

"Ain't nobody dead yet," Glasscock said, throwing the coffee into the snow, making an arcing brown stain. "Gawd, but that was awful stuff. How far do you reckon is that little town with the pretty name?"

"A couple of miles down the valley."

"Reckon they have plenty of dogs there?" he asked.

"Most towns do," I said.

"Then I'll be back," Glasscock said. "Vess, you want to help?"

Vess Akers grinned like an idiot.

"Come on," Glasscock said, laughing. "You can tell your grandchildren about the part you played in the Great Canine Raid of sixty-four. Oh, claws as sharp as sabers! Oh, the flashing teeth!"

Ike nodded as they passed him on their way to saddle the horses.

The thunder shook the ground again, and it seemed to bring more snow from the sky. Oliver Shepherd pushed the brim of his hat back and looked at the sky, then said, "Bill, I've been talking to some of the boys, and we reckon it's time to head for Texas. You know we've always been a democratic organization—hell, that's how you got elected captain—but we'd rather finish the war someplace where the climate is a little warmer."

"I'm surprised, Ol," I said. "I thought you would want to see your family in Nelson County again. And I sure could use you as a scout when we get to the middle of Kentucky."

"Well, my cousin George is staying with you," he said. "He's a good man and knows the country well. Like I said, we took a vote. George was for going home, but I reckon we'd be hounded like rabbits."

"Which of the boys are you taking to Texas?"

He named four or five of the boys, and they included the youngest and most inexperienced. Then Frank James, who had been listening to the conversation, asked Ol if he would take Dingus with him as well.

"If that's what you want," Ol said.

"It is what Ma would want," Frank said. "I don't expect to survive this war, but it would make me feel better knowing that Jesse might. Take him to Texas."

"Hey," Dingus said. "I thought this was run democratic. Nobody asked for my vote."

"Older brothers vote for younger," Frank said.

"That ain't fair," Dingus said.

"Shut up and pack your kit," Frank said. "You're going to Texas."

Dingus cursed and kicked up a spray of snow with the tip of his boot.

"Captain, are you going to let him treat me this way?" he asked.

"I'm disinclined," I said. "It's a family matter."

"Sonuvabitch," Dingus said, becoming more agitated. "This stinks. Someday, Buck, I'll be doing the thinking— and you'll be taking my orders and when you complain, I'll just tell you to shut up."

"O God!" Frank recited—and we knew he was reciting because he used his theatrical voice. *"That one might read the book of fate . . ."*

"Oh, shut up," Dingus said. "I've had my fill of you and your quotes for every damned occasion. I feel like I'm going to pass a great wind, Buck. Do you have a Shakespeare quote for that?"

"Settle down, Jesse," Frank said. "You don't really want to go to Kentucky, and you and Ol Shepherd get along right well. Hell, he's almost more of a brother to you than I am—I've been away fighting the war for most of the time you've been growing up."

Dingus was now so angry he could barely speak.

"Why do I have to go to Texas?" he asked, his eyes filled with tears. "Why can't I just go *home*, Buck? If the war's over, it's over—how am I going to be any better off in Texas than I would be in Clay County?"

"They'd kill you quick," Frank said.

"But at least I'd die at home, Buck . . ."

Jim Little threw me a glance.

I nodded.

". . . and that beats being cornered in some godforsaken patch of sand and scrub called Texas that is thick with wild Indians and rattlesnakes and only God knows what else and being shot down like . . ."

Jim Little moved behind him, drew his Navy, and rapped the barrel expertly on the back of his head. Dingus's eyes fluttered and then rolled back into his head, showing all whites, and his knees buckled.

". . . a dog."

Dingus collapsed into the snow.

"There," Jim Little said. "Now we're square."

Frank scowled.

"He needed hitting," he said, "but did you have to hit him so hard?"

"It was a rock," Jim Little said, pointing to the scar on his forehead. "He hit me with a rock in a snowball. There are rules of engagement, you know. There . . . are . . . *rules*."

An hour later, Oliver Shepherd departed camp with the boys who had voted to go with him, and with Dingus James—who had recovered enough of his senses to sit upright in the saddle. He had exchanged a few kind words with his brother, and he asked that if they were reunited after the war, they never again be separated except by death—and Frank agreed.

"Pass love to my kinfolk," Shepherd called as he was nearly out of sight in the gently falling snow, "and hell to our enemies. Farewell, Charley Quantrill. Watch your back!"

Glasscock and Vess Akers returned not long after. A black dog was slung over the saddle in front of Vess, and the mutt was bright-eyed and its pink tongue lolled from the side of its mouth.

"Damn," Frank said. "Did you have to find such a cute one?"

"It is a very small town," Glasscock said. "We didn't have much of a choice."

"Well, this one looks like it belongs to somebody," Frank said, scratching behind the dog's ears. "Couldn't you find a stray?"

"Like I said," Glasscock said sternly. "It was the only one we could find, and we had a shoot-out in the alley behind the only tavern in town at that."

"Was anybody hurt?" I asked.

"Just feelings," Glasscock said. "The Arkansawyers

presented a strong objection to the theft of their dog, but
we countered with a few well-placed retorts of our own,
which made them seek shelter inside the brick tavern."

"Were you followed?" I asked.

"I think not," Glasscock said, swinging down from his
saddle. "Besides, the snow would have covered our tracks
in a matter of a quarter of an hour." He withdrew his
Arkansas toothpick from his belt and beckoned for Vess
to hand over the dog.

"What're you up to?" Vess asked.

"You know what has to be done for smallpox," Glasscock said. "We slit the dog's throat and smudge Joe's face
with the blood. It only works with a black dog. That's
why we had to find a *black* one. Didn't you wonder why
we were looking for a particular shade?"

"No," Vess said. "I just thought you were looking for
a dog you could find easy in the snow."

"Damn, but you are simple," Glasscock said. "Now
hand over Lucky."

"Lucky?" I asked.

"Yeah," Vess said. "I named him on the ride back. But
it looks like I got that wrong, too."

I sighed.

"Dick," I said, "put your knife away."

"But the dog has to be killed," Glasscock protested.

"No, it doesn't, not now," I said.

"I was hoping Lucky could come with us," the boy
said wistfully.

"We can't have a dog with us, Vess," I said. "We can't
keep it quiet. And I don't even know if we could feed it."

"Please?" Vess asked.

"No," I said. "But we'll leave the dog with the Hall
brothers. It's a good-natured dog, and the warmth of its

body may do Joseph more good on cold winter nights than spilling its blood ever will."

Vess muttered, then nodded resignedly.

Then he glanced around and asked, "Where's Ol' Shepherd and Dingus?"

"Gone to Texas," Frank James said.

"Captain, should I go to Texas?"

"No," I said. "I got you into this war when your mother entrusted me with your care, and I'll get you out. We're headed east to Virginia, where we can join Lee's army and surrender with honor when the time comes."

Book Two

Down in yonder green field
There lies a Knight slain under his shield,
His hounds they lie down at his feet
So well they can their Master keep,
His hawks they fly so eagerly
There no fowl dare come nigh.

—The Three Ravens

The Slough

We crossed the Mississippi on the last night of the year at Devil's Elbow.

The spot is twenty miles or so above Memphis, near the notorious Island No. 37, and is among the least patrolled stretches of the Mississippi because for generations it has been home to river pirates. We didn't find any pirates, but we did find an old yawl that had probably done service on the deck of a steamboat when the river was still host to commercial traffic. The yawl leaked, but the boys patched it with pitch and hemp and we slipped across in the middle of the night, two or three men at a time, with the horses swimming behind.

We nicked the corner of Tennessee and rode generally to the northeast, and on the first day of January, we crossed into Kentucky. Ours wasn't a direct route to Kentucky, but rather a meandering path meant to avoid large concentrations of Yankees. Had we ridden direct from Missouri, we would have crossed the Mississippi at St. Louis and cut straight across Illinois to Louisville, but instead we had to seek the little-traveled and poorly patrolled paths.

Consequently, I don't know exactly where we entered

Kentucky—we were cutting across country and there were few landmarks—but it was somewhere "Between the Rivers," as they say; that is, between the Cumberland and the Tennessee.

The weather continued to be wretched and even though Ol Shepherd's cousin was from Kentucky, he didn't know this part of the state, so we were proceeding blindly. Late one afternoon the column found itself in a slough that seemed without end, and the weather had warmed just enough to turn things to soup. With the ground getting no firmer, I ordered the boys to halt. I gathered Frank James and Jim Little, and told them to scout a few miles to the north and northeast. I would go west, I said. We needed to find a way out if we didn't want to bivouac on the soggy ground. The first one to find a hard path would shoot once into the air, pause five seconds, and fire twice more, to summon the column.

One of us, I assumed, would find a path out.

"I don't like the idea of us splitting up," Jim Little said.

"It's the dead of winter," I said. "I'm cold and tired of being in the saddle and bored. I'd welcome a little trouble, just to vary the routine."

Then I turned Old Charley to the northwest.

Soon the slough became so choked with trees and brambles that I was forced to lean over the neck of my horse in order to pass through, and even to touch my spurs to his flanks to urge him to break through the thicket. I was almost ready to turn back when I glimpsed a clearing up ahead, and pressed Old Charley forward.

Suddenly the thicket was behind us and Old Charley's shoes were ringing on rock. The rocky path bisected the clearing, became a rocky ford at a meandering creek with sharp banks, and then the path ran in front of an old cabin at the far end of the clearing. The cabin had a shake roof and rough sides, built not in the ubiquitous dogtrot style of the West, but as a great one-roomed structure with a gently sloping roof. On the roof was a squad of crows.

A fire was blazing in the yard, and over the fire hung a big black kettle. A young woman was leaning over the kettle, stirring the laundry with a broad wooden paddle, and she wore an old-fashioned outfit in dark colors—a low-cut blouse, a sort of leather vest that laced up the sides. Beneath the hem of her skirt her bare feet darted.

I walked Old Charley across the ford, and his shoes clattered on the stones. I assumed the woman would hear me coming, but as I drew near she did not look up from the laundry. The crows began to crane their heads, shake their wings, and caw rudely.

It seemed to me that the woman was a widow—such a somber, old-fashioned outfit must surely be a symbol of mourning—and that she might be deaf as well. I sat in the saddle for a moment, my hands resting easily on the pommel, and looked around the place. Surely, I thought, this woman isn't alone in the wilderness. There must be someone else about, but I spied no one.

"Pardon me," I said, finally.

The woman glanced up from her work and gave me a knowing smile. She was not yet thirty, and striking—the leather thing accentuated her breasts, her hair was jet-black, and her eyes were pale blue.

"Your clothes," she said. "They are nearly ready."

"No, they cannot be my clothes," I said. "I'm a stranger seeking a course out of the slough—am I on the right path?"

"Aye, you are on the path," she said, then flashed me an inviting smile. I don't remember ever seeing teeth so white. "But there is time yet. I have grain for your horse,

powder and ball for your revolvers, food and whiskey for
you—and more."

"You have mistaken me for someone else," I said.

"No, you're the one," she said, then stirred the pot
more forcefully. "Your clothes are nearly clean, and then
I will lay them upon the line. While they dry you may
pass some time with me."

"My men," I said.

"They will wait."

I dismounted, because I did not want to appear rude.

"Aren't you cold?" I asked, nodding at the bare feet.

She laughed.

"Miss," I said, doffing my hat and looking her directly
in the eyes. "My apologies for being direct, but you are
confused. Can you tell me if this path stays firm and leads
beyond the marshy ground?"

"It does," she said. "And it leads far beyond that."

She moved close to me and gently touched my hair
with her fingertips.

"So fair," she said. "Like cornsilk."

Then she kissed me, and I did not resist. Her lips tasted
peculiar—something reminded me of wild game—and
when I placed a hand behind her head, I found her hair
was unusually coarse. Her body surged against me, and
she pressed her belly against the barrel of the Colt's
Army in my belt. When we broke, I caught my breath and
found wits enough to speak.

"You are wearing black," I said. "Your man—what
happened to your man?"

"My love is here with me now," she said.

"No, you must have a husband, or—"

"I am alone," she said.

"But the clothes . . ."

"They are yours."

She must have been mad, driven mad by grief, although how a madwoman could survive by herself in the middle of such a place is beyond my reason. For a moment I thought about taking her—Who would know? And it had been weeks since I had felt a girl beneath me—but then I recalled the peculiar taste of her lips, and the coarseness of her hair.

"What's your name?" I asked.

"Don't you recognize me?"

She began to loosen the laces on the vest-type thing she wore. Then she pulled it off over her head, and then dropped her skirt. Now she was wearing only the large billowing blouse, and her immodesty shocked me—she wore no undergarments.

"Come," she said, grasping my hand. "Battle will come soon enough. Take my love with you."

I resisted.

"Do you not find me comely?" she asked.

"Comely," I said, amused that she would use the word I had explained to Vess at Tuscumbia. I was also unable to take my eyes from the flesh not hidden by the dark blouse—the curve of a breast, the crown of a nipple, the smooth expanse of thigh. "Of course. But, miss, I can hardly take advantage of you, even if you insist."

"I do more than insist," she said. "I declare for you."

"You don't even know me."

"Oh, I've known you in a hundred desperate situations, and you have won my favor," she said.

"You flatter me," I said. "But you are mistaken."

"My patience is not infinite," she said, her countenance growing stormy. "Take me now"—only the word she used wasn't *take* but something rougher and ordinarily heard only in the speech of men—"or forfeit my affections and harvest the consequences."

"I have no idea of what you're talking about," I said.

"Take me," she said, her lips drawn back to show her teeth. "Here, on the ground—or there, bent over the fence. Draw your pistol, bind my hands, impose your will. I grow excited thinking of my surrender. Take pleasure in my cries. Take me as you took Lawrence."

"What did you say?" I asked, unbelieving.

She took a step forward and snatched the Army from my belt. She fumbled with the gun a bit, then managed to pull the hammer back to full cock. Holding the revolver in both hands, she thrust it forward a couple of times, as if she were taunting me with it.

"What, you're going to shoot me?" I asked.

"Take me," she said, smiling. "Take me, my love."

I stepped forward and slipped one arm around her waist. She melted against me and turned her head back, her mouth slightly parted, and I kissed her roughly, and I felt her tongue graze my teeth. With my free hand, I found the Colt and grasped it by the cylinder, with my index finger beneath the hammer.

Then I jerked away and struck her across the mouth.

Her head snapped back in a spray of black hair, but she did not fall, as I expected. Instead, she planted her bare feet on the cold ground, smeared the blood from the corner of her mouth across her cheek with the back of her hand, and leered at me.

"Yes," she said. "Taste my blood."

She drew near, but I stepped back.

"Turn not away," she warned.

I placed the Army in my belt and retrieved my hat from the ground. Then I put one foot into the stirrup and swung up onto Old Charley.

"You're mad," I said.

The woman was enraged.

"There will be no other chance," she screeched. "Deny me now and I shall have my revenge. When you need me most, I will hinder instead of help—I will trip those once-sure feet, I will render your hand impotent, I will make your death ignoble and remind you of who hath turned your fate."

To the north, there was a pistol shot, a pause, and then two more.

I wheeled Old Charley, splashed across the rocky ford, and spurred him back into the thicket.

Old Charley

I didn't mention the encounter with the madwoman at the ford to Jim Little or any of the boys. What would I say? Besides, I was half convinced it was a dream, something brought on by the monotony of the saddle or perhaps a fever of which I was unaware.

In western Christian County we crossed the tracks of three dozen horses and, hoping to take fresh mounts from Yankee cavalry, followed them. But after just a few miles of hard riding, Old Charley's gait became uneven, and I slowed him to a walk.

Jim Little wheeled his horse and fell in beside me.

"Charley's lame," he said.

"Not yet," I said. "But close to it."

The next morning we found a blacksmith just outside the town of Canton and the boys dismounted and took their rest in the yard. We could hear some hammering going on inside the shop, so Jim Little and I walked Old Charley through the big double doors and found the smithy near the cold forge, working on patching a big black kettle.

He was forty or fifty years old, and thin, although his arms looked like they belonged to a much younger man.

His face was black with grime, which matched his mood, and he barely glanced up at me as I approached.

"I'm Captain Clarke of the Second Colorado—"

"I don't give a damn who you are," the smithy interrupted.

"Pardon?" Jim Little asked in that tone that was anything but cordial.

"You troopers keep on riding," he said. "I don't have time to fix the locks on your guns or make you a knife with a foot-long blade or any of the other foolishness that goes into the killing of men."

Jim Little pulled his Navy.

I pushed the barrel down and shook my head. Grudgingly, Jim Little slipped the revolver back into his belt.

"My horse," I said. "I'd be grateful if you could take a look."

The blacksmith looked at Old Charley, who was holding his right hoof a few inches from the sawdust floor.

"Horses," he said. "That's different."

The smithy threw down the rasp and stood.

As he approached Old Charley, the horse backed away with a nicker.

"Careful," I warned. "He's a bit mean-tempered."

"Bullshit," the smithy said.

As the smithy reached for the bridle, the horse lunged and tried to bite him. The blacksmith drew his hand away just in time and flexed his fingers, just to make sure they were all there.

"Damn you," the smith said.

"Do not curse my horse," I said, and rested my right hand on the back strap of my Army revolver.

"Not him," the smithy said. "You. What have you done to this animal?"

He carefully placed a hand on Old Charley's muzzle,

looked deep into his dark eyes, and made some type of soothing sounds deep in his throat. Then he reached into a pocket of his apron and brought out an apple and allowed Old Charley to eat it from his palm.

"Humans don't understand horses," the smithy said. "Unlike us, these animals hate conflict. Sometimes just riding them presents a conflict for these proud animals, and often we ask them to do terrible things—to help kill each other, in fact, or to run another horse into the ground. In response, they bite and buck and try to make us leave them alone. They may turn mean, but they really don't want to."

"And I suppose the horses have told you all of this," Jim Little said.

"What kind of idiot are you?" the smithy asked. "Horses don't talk. That's just one of the advantages they have over the human race. But I've spent years getting to know them and even though they don't talk, they communicate. You just have to know what to listen for."

The smithy touched Old Charley's cheek affectionately. "What's his name?"

I told him.

Then he knelt and ran his hands over the right foreleg, lifted the hoof, and inspected the shoe and the frog.

"It's swollen," he said. "You can feel the heat."

"Don't have to feel it," I said. "I can see it."

"How long's he been favoring this leg?"

"A year or more," I said.

"Oh, Charley," the smithy said to the horse. "You're in pain, aren't you, cousin?"

"Is it his shoe?" I asked.

"His shoe ain't doing him much good," he said. "But no, it's not the shoe. The problem is in his hoof. The coffin bone is in bad shape, and it's just going to get worse if you keep riding him hard."

"Can you do anything for him?"

"Well, I can build him a shoe that will help restore the balance a bit," the smithy said. "But he's just going to get worse and worse. Every time he puts his weight on that foot, the pain for him is unbearable—but he continues to do it because he doesn't want to let you down."

Jim Little shook his head.

"So you're saying he's worthless as a war mount?" he asked the smithy.

"He's not useless," the smithy said. "No horse is useless. If you're careful, he'll go another year or two without getting any worse. But ride him hard, and he'll be lame in a month."

"I'm sorry, Bill," Jim Little said. "It looks like Old Charley is finished."

"Some said you were finished back at Fayette, when you were shot through both hips," I said. "You limp a little now, but do you feel like you're finished? Do you think I shouldn't have gone back for you just because Anderson said your race had been run?"

"You know I am forever grateful," Jim Little said. "But we're talking about an animal here. If he can't charge and cut in battle, then he's a liability."

"Horses are more than animals," the smithy said. "They're our better kin, and that's why we don't eat horseflesh except in cases of starvation, and sometimes not even then. Damn the French and their cannibal tastes."

"You are touched, ain't you?" Jim Little asked.

"Leave Old Charley here with me," the smithy said. "I'll care for him."

"No," I said. "I want him with me. He's my luck. Besides, in a few weeks or months we'll be home."

"Thought you said you were from Colorado," the smithy said.

"I mean, the Rebels are all but beaten. The war will be over soon and we can head for home. Once we get there, Old Charley will never have to work or fight again."

The smithy nodded.

"Fix up that special shoe, won't you?" I asked. "When you're done with the kettle, I mean."

"Hell, I'll do it now," the smithy said. "I don't know why I'm trying to patch this junk, anyway. There's damned little to cook in it."

A Busted Pot

W̲e continued to the north and east, and Old Charley seemed to do a bit better with the special shoe the blacksmith had made for him. By and by we crossed into Muhlenberg County. Not far from the Green River, we came upon a farmhouse hard upon the side of a wooded hill.

It was about dark and the boys were hungry and they asked me if they could approach the cabin and attempt to persuade the occupants to rustle up a little dinner.

"Maybe we can sleep in their barn," Jim Little said. His face was pale and he spoke through tight lips, and his hat was pulled down low and the drizzling rain was dripping from the brim. "My old hips are troubling me a bit. A nap in a pile of straw would seem as nice as a night in a feather bed."

At the edge of a barren field, I stood in the stirrups and took a look through the field glasses. I was being jostled a bit because he kept favoring that right hoof, and it was hard to keep the glasses still enough to actually discern anything, so I slipped down from the saddle and stood with my boots planted on the hard ground.

The farmhouse had a broad porch and smoke was curling from the chimney and it was drizzling rain and miserable cold. It looked about like a hundred other little houses we had come upon in four years of war, so I gave my consent. While I watched through the glasses, Jim Little rode forward with a squad that included Honey John Noland and Peyton Long and Frank James.

Jim Little stopped twenty yards from the porch. He had pulled one of his Navies but held it casually, his hand crossed on the pommel.

"Hello the house," he said.

Every window on the porch gushed white smoke.

Jim Little's roan stumbled and went down, spilling its rider onto the winter ground. I saw the revolver fly from his grip and land a few feet away. Honey John and Peyton Long and Frank James returned fire with a few off-hand shots as they wheeled their horses and dashed for the relative safety of a woodpile and an old wagon.

"Dammit," I said, and touched my heels to Old Charley's flanks.

He surged forward, and the rest of the boys followed me. We thundered across the field and poured lead into the windows and door of the cabin as we came. By the time we reached Jim Little, the door had been reduced to a sliver of wood hanging on its iron hinges.

The boys formed a half circle around us as I slid down from Old Charley. I knelt on the ground beside Jim Little and touched his shoulder.

"Where're you hit?"

Jim Little's face was twisted in pain, but he managed a smile.

"Through the hip," he said. "Where the hell else? I can't feel much, Captain. That's how it was at Fayette—it didn't hurt, at least not at first. It just feels warm and numb and wet. Would you take a look and tell me how bad it is?"

He was lying on his side, propping himself up by his left arm, and his right thigh was covered in blood. He turned his head away as I took my knife and slit his trousers so I could get a better look. There was an ugly black pucker the size of my thumb high up on his leg, near his hip, and the ball must have nicked an artery because every couple of seconds bright red blood would spurt from the wound. I didn't see an exit wound, so the ball must have clattered around his pelvis and broken things up like a hammer thrown into a stack of dishes.

"Well?" Jim Little asked.

"I've seen worse," I said, thinking of Lawrence. I took my kerchief and wadded it up and pressed it in the wound to stanch the blood. "We're going to move you out of the line of fire and deal with these bastards that did this to you."

"Bill," Jim Little said. "I'd have done it to them first."

"Get him out of here," I told the boys, and two of them grabbed Jim Little by the collar and dragged him over behind the woodpile where Honey John stood with his Sharps. Then I walked toward the cabin, my hands empty.

"Who's in the cabin?" I demanded.

There was no answer, but I could hear movement inside.

"You'd better talk to me," I said. "You're outnumbered."

"Go to hell," somebody shouted in a voice like sandpaper.

"In time," I said. "But send me there now and these boys won't kill you quick—they'll make sure you suffer. You sons of bitches have shot my best friend without provocation, and you will pay."

"Without provocation?" the gruff voice came back. "You're guerrillas."

"All Jim Little wanted was a meal and a place to sleep," I said. "I'm guessing you're not a happy farm family, judging from the number of rifle shots that came from the cabin."

"What are you doing?" Peyton Long asked in a strangled whisper as he strode in front of me. "Let's kill them and be done."

"Would you care to command?" I asked in a low voice.

"No, Captain, I just—"

"Then stand aside, won't you?"

Peyton nodded and stepped away.

"You in the cabin," I called. "What are you, a foraging party?"

"Yes," the voice came.

"How many?"

"Twelve," came the reply.

"I reckon that means six," I said. "Where're your horses?"

"Behind the barn."

"Good," I said. "We need new mounts."

"So that's it?" the voice called.

"What else is there?" I asked. "I would advise you not to shoot into a superior force next time, but there won't be a next time. Ever seen anybody burned alive? Well, you're about to experience it firsthand. Peyton!"

"Yes, Captain?"

"Gather some things to burn the cabin," I said. "And, boys, anybody who runs from the cabin while it's on fire, I want you to shoot them in the legs and then throw them back into the blaze."

"That's a splendid order," Peyton said.

"How's Jim Little?" I asked.

"Bleeding like a hog," Honey John said. "But still with us."

A minute or so passed while Peyton and the boys started kicking an old shed apart for use as kindling. I knew the men inside the cabin were huddled together and considering whether to shoot me where I stood and try to make a run for it or try to talk their way out of it.

"May we ask your name?" the gruff voice called.

"Captain Quantrill," I said.

"Quantrill," the voice came back. "Of Missouri?"

"The same," I said. "Where should we send word of your demise?"

"Illinois," came the reply. "We're from Macon County, most of us. There's my brother and me—"

"No, I'll never remember all of your names," I said. "Throw something out, a paper or a chunk of wood, with them written upon it."

"How badly is your friend hurt?"

"He took one of your rifle balls through the hips," I said.

The boys were piling wood on the porch.

"Anybody have some coal oil?" Frank James asked.

The boys said they had none.

"How about you Yankees in there?" Frank asked. "Any full lamps you could pass out to us?"

"We think not," the voice said.

"Well, that's all right," Frank said. "We'll make do."

Vess Akers took a rag from his pocket, thumbed back the lever on his gunpowder flask, and shook some powder into it. Then he stuffed the rag in the base of the pile of wood. Some of the other boys stuffed old newspaper and bits of paper or other combustible trash around the rag.

"When this gets going," Peyton told the boys, "grab a

burning stick and take it over the sides and back of the cabin. The aim is to roast all sides evenly. Otherwise, you get everybody bunched up in a knot in the corner that don't burn, and they die of suffocation. It just takes the fun out of it."

Peyton stuck the barrel of his revolver into the base of the kindling and fired. The shower of sparks set fire to the rag, which whizzed and flared. The newspapers and trash caught fire, and the blaze soon ignited the kindling.

In a minute or two the fire was going right well, and licking up the side of the cabin. I imagine smoke and perhaps a little flame were seeping in through the chinks. At least, the smoke would be pooling in the rafters.

"Captain Quantrill," the voice called.

"What is it, Illinois?"

"We might be able to help each other."

"How's that?"

There was a pause, and the sounds of an argument. I could hear the gruff voice telling a couple of the boys the way it was going to be.

"Captain," the voice called finally. "We're sorry for shooting your friend yonder, and we would undo it if we could. But that's now a busted pot. What we can do is get your friend to a surgeon."

"What do you want in return?" I asked.

"Well, not to roast if we don't have to," the voice said. "And a promise you won't shoot us as we come out that door. Put out that fire, leave your friend with us, and we'll see that he gets to a hospital. We have a wagon in the barn, along with the team. We'll make an ambulance out of it for him."

I motioned for the fire to be extinguished, and Frank James stepped forward and kicked the flaming bundle off the porch and into the yard. The side of the cabin was still ablaze, however, and some of the boys began smothering it with a blanket.

"Come out the door," I said. "Leave your guns inside."

A sergeant appeared in the doorway. He was twenty-five or thirty, and had a full beard, and when he was certain we weren't going to shoot him, he stepped forward. Behind him came four others, all private soldiers, and they seemed very young to me.

"Where are the people who live here?"

"Don't know," the sergeant said. "It was empty when we got here. We were cold, and there was firewood here already cut in the yard, so it seemed like a good idea."

"Where's your main force?"

"Not much of a force," the sergeant said. "A company only, ten miles away in Greenville. They've been detailed to protect the town. They were running short on meat, so the captain sent us out to shoot some game. We haven't seen a damn thing except you."

"Carry Jim Little into the cabin," I told the boys.

They spread a blanket beside him and rolled him gently onto it, but Jim Little let out a groan that sounded like air escaping from the bellows of a concertina when you knock it over by accident. Three men got on each side of him and took him into the cabin, where they put him on a pallet they found in the corner. A rough army blanket was thrown over him.

I followed, then sat on a stool next to Jim Little.

Honey John came in with the Navy, brushed the dirt from it, and placed it on Jim Little's stomach. My friend slipped the gun beneath the rough blanket, then looked over at me and grinned.

"My race is run," he said. "It's been one helluva ride, hasn't it? We've spilled a lot of blood together, and thankfully most of it has belonged to others. A truer friend a man could not ask for, and I am grateful for that."

"No need for that kind of talk," I said. "You're going to the hospital at Greenville, and you'll be treated well or I will know the reason why. When you're well enough to ride, you slip out and head for home."

"Don't trust these Yankees," he said. "I'm dead—you know that. They have killed me, but that was their duty. But now you have shared your identity with them and once you and the boys ride off, they won't be able to keep their mouths shut. Soon you'll be hounded across Kentucky. Bill, there is no reason for you to trust them, and I don't want you being hunted like a dog because you tried to save my life."

He held out his hand, the one with the stub for a middle finger, and I clasped it in both of mine. Our eyes met, and I held his gaze for a long time. The crow's-feet at the corners of his blue eyes were deeper than I remembered, and his temples were dappled with gray.

"We can trust these Illinois boys," I assured him.

"I'd like to meet the one what shot me," Jim Little said. "Do you think I could do that, Bill? I just want to see his face. Also, do you think I could have a little water? My mouth is so damned dry I feel like I'm spitting sand."

I called for the sergeant and asked him to fetch his canteen, and to summon the man who had shot Jim Little. The sergeant handed me the canteen, but asked what I wanted with the private soldier he called Hallstrom.

"My friend wants to talk to him."

"All right," the sergeant said uneasily, and called for the private.

I clasped Jim Little on the shoulder, then stood. He called for the private, who walked into the cabin while I was walking out. The boy was eighteen or perhaps nineteen, with a crow's nest of brown hair and ears that stuck on either side of his head like signal flags.

On the porch, Frank James was leaning against one of the posts, his thumbs hooked in his belt, gazing toward the southwestern horizon.

"Trouble?" I asked.

I looked in that direction, but saw no dust or smoke. The sun had set but there was still a smudge of daylight in the west, and the evening star hung like a glittering jewel against the chill sky.

"No," Frank said. "I was just thinking about Dingus and whether he made it to Texas or not, and if he did what trouble he's found there. That boy's a loaded pistol with a hair trigger. You think much about your family, Bill?"

"Not often," I said.

"You're lucky," Frank said. "There's my old mother up at the home place in Clay County, taking care of our simpleminded little brother and Dr. Samuel, who was hung by the Yankees until he was nearly dead. Mother was pregnant with my little sister at the time, and the Federals forced her to watch the hanging, and they whipped Dingus so harshly that everyone feared he would die for lack of blood. I reckon that's what made him turn so deadly and peculiar."

"And what is your excuse?" I asked.

"I read too damned much," Frank said. "Captain, what's your pleasure?"

"We'll spend the night," I told him. "But I want out of here before dawn. Tell the boys to see to their horses before sleeping. Take whatever feed is in the barn, but leave the Yankee horses be—we want them to keep their team so they can take poor Jim Little to Greenville."

"How is he?"

"He'll pull through," I said, aware that Jim Little was within earshot. "He has before."

Frank stepped off the porch to relay the orders.

There were a couple of Yankees standing in the yard off by themselves, talking, and regarding the Missouri boys with suspicion. Neither held a rifle, and one of them had produced a new clay pipe from his pocket. The pipe was already packed with tobacco, and he struck a match with his thumb and held it to the bowl.

Honey John was sitting on the edge of the porch, the Sharps across his lap.

Another of the Yankee privates was sitting beside him, and he was talking to John in low tones. The private's Springfield rifle was propped casually beside him, the butt resting on the ground. The private had earnest green eyes and straw-colored hair, and he was explaining how he was an abolitionist, how his family had maintained a stop on the Underground Railroad, and why Honey John ought to leave us and go back to Greenville with them.

Honey John threw his head back and laughed.

The private recoiled in offense.

"Tell the captain," Honey John said.

"Well, it was a private conversation," the private said.

"He thinks I'm a slave," Honey John told me.

"Aren't you one of these fellows' cook?" the private said. "Or man? Not a slave exactly, but . . . you are in some manner of servitude."

"I am a free man of color," Honey John said.

"Lincoln has made you so," the boy said with a glad smile. "The Proclamation of Emancipation—"

"Let me explain this in a way that you can understand," Honey John said. "My home is Missouri. Say that I was still a slave there. Would that proclamation make me a freeman? No, it wouldn't. And it wouldn't if I lived here in Kentucky, either. Mr. Lincoln freed only those slaves in the states that are in rebellion, not in border or Union states. So, how many souls did he actually liberate? What kind of courage does it take to emancipate a country which is not in your command?"

"But the peculiar institution is intolerable," the private protested.

"Which peculiar institution would that be?" Honey John asked. "Slavery? Of course it is horrible. It is cruel beyond imagination, but then so is war. But what drives slavery and war and every other evil thing you can imagine? Politics. When politicians talk war, they make it sound like the most glorious enterprise ever devised by man, and just the opposite is true. Politics is the most peculiar institution of all, where you see a thing painted blue and call it red."

"That makes no sense," the boy said.

"Call a thing red long enough and you'll have a great many people rush to agree with you," Honey John said, "and there will be a clamor to get a law passed to have the name of blue forever changed to red, and after the bill is passed it will be against the law to refer to the blue sky or the deep blue ocean or the blue eyes of your own true love. But no matter how much the preachers and politicians talk about the beautiful red sky or the crimson ocean or the scarlet eyes of your sweetheart, it won't change the truth."

The private drew his knees up and rested his chin upon them.

"Some men will always be free, no matter what a piece of paper says," Honey John said as he stood. "When I was in bondage to the Noland family, I knew in my heart I was free. And over the years of my servitude I was like an uncle to those two boys standing over there, though they are men now. While I hated the peculiar institution, I came to love those boys, and the family treated me with nothing but kindness. When they lost their home to the Jayhawkers, and they could no longer feed me, they set me free—and I chose to stay and fight because when the bastards burned the Noland home, they were burning my home, too."

"I had not thought of that," the boy said. "But that example is too specific. There is a generality to be considered here, a principle. You must recognize the harm you do by taking up arms for those who enslave you."

"A principle didn't burn my home," Honey John said. "Yankees did. And the Noland family set me free. Let me ask a question, my young friend: Would you let me fight with your outfit?"

"Well, if it were up to me, but it ain't."

"Yankees don't let coloreds fight alongside them," Honey John said. "But all right, I'll take you at your word. You would let me fight alongside you. But, honey, do you have a sister?"

"Yes," the Yankee boy said. "She is a fine young woman and writes to me every week and includes bits of ribbon and cards with inspirational verses. She can recite all of John Greenleaf Whittier's poem 'Le Marais Du Cygne' in a fine voice upon request."

"How sweet," Honey John said. "Now, how would you feel about me courting your sister?"

"I would object," the boy said.

"Of course you would," Honey John said. "But you're protesting for the wrong reasons. You should object because I am a hard man with a large-bore carbine who has sworn his fealty to a bunch of murderers and thieves. But you object because of the color of my skin."

"You are the must peculiar nigger I have ever met," the boy said indignantly.

Then there was a pistol shot inside the cabin, and reflexively I turned to look through the open doorway. Another shot lit up the interior of the cabin like a flash of summer lightning, and the sergeant came staggering through the doorway, his hands clasping his throat, and blood pouring from between his fingers. A horrid strangling sound was coming from his open mouth.

The abolitionist boy snatched up his Springfield and tried to bring it to bear on Honey John, but the barrel was too long to clear one of the posts that held the roof over the porch. The Sharps was in Honey John's big hands in a moment, and he fired from the hip. The blast of the Sharps sounded like an artillery piece and it spat embers like a Roman candle. The ball struck the boy in the stomach and knocked him off the porch into the yard, where he lay with his dead eyes toward the stars and the blouse over his stomach scorched and smoldering.

Then Honey John took the Sharps by the barrel and, swinging it like a bat, struck the back of the sergeant's head with the stock. The impact made a singing sound, like when you drive an ax into a hard stump and the handle stings your hands, and the sergeant fell dead on the porch with the back of his head stove in.

Frank James came tearing around the corner, a pistol in each hand.

"What the hell?" he asked.

I looked out into the yard, but did not see the pair of Yankees that had been standing there just moments before. The clay pipe was on the ground, the bowl was broken, and the ball of tobacco glowed cherry red.

"Find the Yankees," I said. "Kill them."

Then two more pistol shots came from inside the cabin.

I drew and cocked my revolver and rushed into the cabin, where I saw Jim Little sitting up, the smoking Navy in his hand. At his feet lay the boy called Hallstrom, the one who had shot Jim Little, dead from a pistol shot that punctured the bridge of his nose. In the corner another Yankee was crumpled, his arms folded tightly over his chest.

"Jimmie!" I called.

"Sorry, Bill," he said. "It's better this way."

Then he pressed the end of the octagonal barrel of the Navy against his right temple and pulled the trigger. The revolver bucked and Jim Little's hair puffed on the other side of his head and the ball knocked a splinter from the wall behind him. Then he slumped over, the gun clattered on the floor, and the pistol ball—which had passed through Jim Little's skull, bounced off the oak panel, then ricocheted off the far wall—rolled across the planks, and came to rest against the toe of my left boot.

All of this last took but an instant, but to my shocked senses time was flowing as slowly as sorghum syrup. At the same time, I felt paralyzed, unable to move, and while my mind was rushing forward to knock the gun from Jim Little's hand, I was as still as if my feet had been nailed to the floor.

"You all right, Captain?" Honey John asked from the door.

I couldn't answer. My throat was swelled shut and my chest was tight and I felt like I was drowning, but could not take a breath. Jim Little was dead. Blood dripped from his long hair onto the floor and bits of brain and bone were spattered on the wall behind him.

Honey John leaned the Sharps against the wall and

came over and placed his rough hand inside my jacket and felt for blood.

"Where're you hit?" he asked.

I shook my head, still unable to breathe.

Honey John took the Army from my hand as I slid to the floor. I plucked the pistol ball from the floor and held it tightly in my right hand while tears began to spill down my cheeks.

"Don't do that, honey," John said, grasping my collar and pulling me to my feet. "You can't let the boys see you like this. Take a breath, say farewell to your friend, and carry on."

Then Honey John threw his arms around my chest and hugged me until I could stand it no longer, and when he released me I found myself sucking in a great torrent of air.

Then he walked over and kicked the Navy away from Jim Little's body.

Hank Noland came through the door and surveyed the carnage with eyes as large as goose eggs. He looked at me, saw the tears on my cheeks, and looked quickly away.

"The Yankees killed Jim with his own gun," Honey John said, tucking the Army in my sash. Then he picked up the Sharps and pulled me toward the door. "But Jim got one of them first, and the captain killed the other two."

"What do we do now?" Hank asked.

"Burn the cabin," Honey John said. "And pray to sweet Jesus for the boys to find and kill that pair of Yankees that ran away."

A Damned Easy Job

It's hard to chase somebody in the dark, especially when you don't have dogs, and Frank James found and dispatched only one of the Yankees. By the time he got back, the cabin was in flames, and the boys were getting ready to ride.

And ride we did.

We headed northeast, following a path that was generally parallel to the Ohio River, fifty miles to the north. We encountered more Federals as we closed the distance to Louisville, and we presented ourselves as the Second Colorado, guerrilla hunters, and were fed and resupplied and helped along by guides who were only too pleased to lead us to the next landmark or crossing or unprotected village. Jim Little's death had made my heart flinty toward all humanity, and we routinely killed these good Samaritans and left their bodies in ditches or heavy timber, where they would freeze and perhaps not be discovered until spring. Often I would consult the maps our unwitting guides bequeathed to us, and assured myself that we were still angling toward Ohio, although I kept my own counsel about that.

As we moved deeper into central Kentucky, the land

began to change, and the rolling hills made it seem as if the horizon was closing in on me. Out West, the prairies were so flat the sky was like a great bowl, and it made one feel small and unimportant in the scheme of Creation. In Kansas and Missouri, where the terrain ranged from flat to foothills, I felt most comfortable; there were trees and rivers and other things against which a man could take the measure of himself. In Kentucky, the grassy hills were bunched together like a rumpled green blanket, and the trees clustered in the streams and hollers, and the earth was rich and black.

We passed about thirty miles south of Louisville and then, because of the increasingly heavy Yankee presence there, we took an easterly bearing, and by the end of January we made Hustonville in Lincoln County. We rode into town at dawn wearing our Federal uniforms and, politely explaining that we needed fresh animals with which to chase the damned guerrillas, were directed to a fine stable owned by a rich man named Weatherford. There, the boys gathered a dozen or so of the best animals while I took my ease in a chair on the porch of the town's only hotel, which was next to the stable.

Allen Parmer had taken a particularly fine gray mare and was riding her out of the stable doors when a young fool in civilian feathers came tearing down the street and ordered Parmer to stop. Behind him were a couple of older men that I took to be kin because they had the same thin nose and sharp chin as the young man doing all of the complaining.

"Who the hell are you?" Parmer asked.

Parmer was young and hot-blooded, and may have been the youngest of the guerrillas riding with me at the time. He certainly had the shortest fuse.

"I am the master of that animal," the young man said,

"and your superior officer. My name is George Cunningham and I served two years as a lieutenant in the Thirteenth Kentucky Cavalry and you shall not take my
horse."

"I see neither the master of this animal nor of me,"
Parmer remarked.

"If that horse leaves this stable," Cunningham vowed,
"it will be over my dead body."

"That is a damned easy job," Parmer said.

He drew the Remington revolver from his belt and shot
the young man in the face. Cunningham crumpled to the
ground, his head a bloody mess, and his father and uncle
began to raise a hue and cry.

I sprang out of the chair and was up on Old Charley in
a moment while shouting for the boys to gather round.
Parmer sent a couple of shots in the direction of the griev-
ing relatives to shut them up, then touched the mare's
flanks and the horse shot forward into the street.

"Dammit," I remarked to Allen Parmer. "You should
have let the idiot have his horse and taken another."

"I wanted this one," Parmer said. "Besides, he insulted
my person."

"I hope your honor has been repaired," I said, "for we
will pay a high price for it soon; by nightfall we shall
have every Yankee in a hundred miles in pursuit of us."

We raced out of town to the north.

By noon we reached Danville, where we made no pre-
tense of being anything but guerrillas. We destroyed the
telegraph office, stole more horses, and robbed what lo-
cals we could find on the street. Some of the boys got particularly fine boots from one local shop. At the hotel, I
commandeered a table in the dining room that faced
the street, and drank coffee while I read the Louisville
papers.

Fort Fisher—the Gibraltar of the South—had fallen. It was the last open port for the blockade runners supplying Lee's army, and its loss was just another nail in the coffin for the Confederacy.

"Is there any funny news?" Vess Akers asked.

"If there is, I can't find it," I said.

Then Frank James tapped on the window glass.

"You'd better come quick, Bill," he said.

"Yankees?" I asked.

"I'll be damned if I know what it is."

I threw down the newspaper, exited the hotel, and stepped out onto the hard dirt street, where the boys were watching a half dozen riders coming into town from the Perryville Pike. In front was a small rider with long brown hair and a broad face and a wide hat with a foxtail affixed to the band.

"Who is that?" I asked.

Frank James just shook his head.

"Form a line," I said.

One of the townspeople that had been too poor to rob was sitting in a rocking chair on the porch of the hotel, wrapped in a dirty blanket, watching the proceedings. He was an old man with a wrinkled face and a tongue that seemed to be caged by his few remaining yellow teeth, and he snorted with laughter.

"You Missouri fellows don't know sic 'em, do you?"

"Explain yourself," I said.

"Why, that's Sue Mundy."

The riders approached with a casual ease, unconcerned they were badly outnumbered, or that one of them was a cripple; his left sleeve was empty and pinned to his jacket. The boy riding in front walked his horse right up to me, smiled broadly, then swung down from the saddle.

He was young, eighteen or nineteen, and short, perhaps five foot four or five, but appeared definitively male.

"Captain Quantrill?" he asked.

"Sue Mundy?" I returned.

"Some call me that," the boy said. "My real name is Jerome Clark."

He removed his gloves, stepped forward, and we clasped hands.

"You are surprised by my gender?"

I nodded.

"Don't believe everything you read in the newspapers," he said. "The editors have taken a nickname I was given in jest long ago to torment the Yankee occupiers. Everyone loves to read about the fair bandit. Besides, what could be more humiliating than being outwitted by a girl?"

"Before the war, I could think of none," I said. "But now I could name half a dozen without pausing for breath."

"Well, you have certainly whacked the hornets' nest this time," he said. "Old Man Weatherford, the man who owns the stable you robbed, has ridden to Stanford, where he delivered the news to the Federal garrison. You have a head start of three or perhaps four hours on a company of Yankee cavalry led by Captain Jim Bridgewater that has been dispatched to chase you."

"I am grateful for the warning," I said.

"We are brothers," he said. "Now tell me, what word do you have of Terrell?"

I told him that I did not know the name.

The boy looked at me strangely.

"Truly you don't know?" he asked. "Why, he's been hired to kill you."

*   *   *

Over coffee at my window table, Sue Mundy told me that Ed Terrell was a twenty-year-old liar and thief and sometime circus performer from Shelby County who had been hired by the Yankees to hunt guerrillas in general and to kill me in particular. Terrell had served in some Yankee volunteer mounted infantry unit, Mundy said, but had been arrested for stealing, and spent most of the war in a stockade before being released and mustered out at the end of December. A few days later, Terrell and his gang were placed on the Federal payroll as guerrilla hunters. They donned red shell jackets, he said, as a signal that no quarter would be given.

"Jennison did the same with his Jayhawkers," I said, "but instead of jackets it was red morocco leggings. Red jackets, black flags. My God, where do these people get their storybook notions?"

"At least it makes him easy to spot," Mundy said, casually drawing a cigar from inside his jacket. He offered another to me, but I declined. He struck a match on the wooden table.

"So, how *did* you get that nickname?"

Mundy stuck the match to the end of the cigar and sucked vigorously.

"Some foolishness back home in Simpson County before the war," he said finally. "Having to do with a girl and a horse and a case of mistaken identity. It means nothing to me now, but the nickname has stuck."

"And how did war find you?"

"It found me quite suddenly on Valentine's Day of 1862 at Fort Donelson on the Cumberland," he said. "I was with the Orphan Brigade and will never forget the hellish sound when the river batteries opened up against the Union gunboats, or how strange the snow and ice seemed when the tubes were belching such fire. And although we beat the Yankees on the water, we could not hold the fort against Grant's ground advance. When General Buckner surrendered four days later at the Dover Inn, I was taken prisoner and was sent to a Federal camp in Indiana."

"And then?"

"I escaped," he said coolly.

"How?"

"It doesn't matter now," he said. "I made my way back in time to ride with John Morgan during his famous raid, and after he was killed in Tennessee, some of us who had ridden together formed our own band."

"Does that include the one-armed invalid that rides with you?"

"I would not call Sam Berry that to his face," Mundy said. "He was Morgan's color sergeant, distinguished himself for valor, and is unequalled by any able-bodied man for pure viciousness."

"And the others," I said. "They rode with Morgan as well?"

Mundy nodded.

"What say we throw in together?"

"Why?" he asked.

"You know the country," I said. "And I have the experience."

Mundy exhaled a cloud of smoke.

"By dark you'll have your hands full," he said. "You'd best find a spot and make your stand. But in a day or two, if you're alive and still game, we will see what mischief we can make together."

Thirty minutes later, the Missouri boys and I tore out of town on the Perryville Pike to the west while Sue Mundy and his fellows went east. A few miles outside of town, we left the pike and darted to the north, picking up the road to Harrodsburg.

We rode for a few hours, until the winter shadows became long on the ground. Then, a few miles south of Harrodsburg, I drew the boys together for a war council.

"We'd best split up," I said. "I have no doubt that the Yankees are hard upon us, and if they catch us together they will surround us and call for reinforcements and kill us at their leisure."

"Wouldn't it be better to stick together and fight it out?" Vess Akers asked.

"This isn't a fight we can win," I said. "There's a whole company of Yankees behind us. Even if it were only two against one, I'd say stand and fight. But this is three of their men to every one of ours."

"By splitting up," Frank James said, "it gives the groups that don't tangle with the Yankees a better chance of getting away. But it will only work if each group agrees not to come to the aid of the others."

But Honey John Noland did not like the plan.

"Captain, I have a queer feeling about this coming fight," he said. "For once, I have to say that Vess Akers has discerned the kernel of wisdom, that we are better together than we are separately. We should keep moving. The Yankees here are different than the Yankees in Missouri."

"What do you mean?" Hank Noland asked.

"They're smarter," Honey John said. "Or better organized. Do you remember the last time the Federals were crawling up our tails in so short a time? It was after we burned Lawrence and Major Preston Plumb chased us down the military road to Fort Scott. That time, we killed a couple of hundred men and burned the whole damned town. This time, we've killed one man and stolen a few horses."

"We can't run forever, John," I said.

"That's true, Captain," he said. "So maybe it's time to surrender."

Nobody spoke for a few moments.

"What do you suppose would happen to us?" Vess Akers asked.

"We'd face execution," I said. "I read in the papers back at Danville that Stephen Burbridge, the commander of the Department of Kentucky at Louisville, has issued general orders that whenever an unarmed Union citizen is killed, four guerrillas will be shot to death in retaliation. Now, which four of you are willing to die for the Yankee that Allen Parmer shot at the stable in Hustonville?"

"To hell with that," Clark Hockensmith said. "I'm with the captain on this. We split up, and the squad the Yankees encounter first keeps them busy while the rest of us get away."

"But we don't keep running," Dick Glasscock said. "We hit someplace they're not expecting, and we hit them hard."

The boys cheered.

"Then I'll take my leave now," Honey John said. "That is, if you don't mind, Captain."

"You know you don't have to ask me, John," I said. "If anybody has lost confidence in my command, they are free to leave."

"I have not lost confidence in you, Captain," he said. "You're the best cavalry commander in the West, and probably the entire damned world. What I have lost confidence in is the numbers—there are just too many Yankees and not enough of us anymore."

Then Honey John addressed his former masters, Hank and Bill Noland.

"Boys," he said, "you've been my family for as long as I can remember. I watched you grow up and I couldn't love you any more had I been your real white uncle. And I hope you will take my counsel seriously when I say it is time to hang up your guns. Come with me and we'll try a run for Texas."

Hank Noland turned his head and wiped a tear from the corner of his eye with the back of his hand. He glanced over at William, whose eyes were also glistening with tears.

"We can't, Honey John," Hank Noland said. "There's nothing for us left in Missouri and there's damned little of Texas I've seen that I would want for my own."

"You feel the same way, William?"

"I'll stay with my brother," Bill Noland said. "But my prayers will be with you."

Honey John nodded, then offered his Sharps to Hank.

"I won't be needing this," he said. "A colored man traveling alone with a big gun is asking for trouble. But I'd appreciate it if you'd swap me for one of those little Colts that I can tuck into my boot should I need it."

Hank handed over the revolver, and Bill gave him a powder flask, a palm full of shot, and some percussion caps. Then Honey John clasped the hands of first one Noland boy, and then the other.

"You get through this war and come look for me in the Red River Valley near the old Mineral Creek camp," he said. "We'll start over and build something with our hands instead of tearing things apart."

Then he touched his fingers to the brim of his hat.

"Deo Vindici," he said.

"Yes," I said. "God will indeed vindicate."

Then Honey John touched his heels to the flanks of his horse. He left the road and headed across the fields to the southwest, where the evening star was shining brightly in the cold January sky.

We formed three groups of about a dozen men each. I led the first group, Frank James took the second, and John Barker had the third. We fanned out across the countryside and found farmhouses a few miles apart where we got supper at gunpoint and waited to see where the Yankees would strike. They found Barker's squad first, and when I heard the shooting in the distance, I ordered the boys to mount up—and ride in the opposite direction.

"It doesn't seem right," Dick Glasscock said, baring his cannibal teeth in the moonlight. "But I'll swallow it."

"Well, I can't," Chad Renick said. "Good luck, boys."

He turned his horse and rode toward the sound of gunfire.

Killed that night were John Barker, Foss Key, Hank Noland, and Chad Renick. The survivors of Barker's squad—some of them badly wounded—were thrown into the stockade at Lexington while the Yankees argued about who among them they were going to execute. Vess Akers, who had been uninjured during the Harrodsburg fight, was among them.

At last, I had made good on my promise to get him out of the war.

The Airdrie Chief

On the second day of February, I combined forces with Sue Mundy and we hit a little town called Midway, which appropriately is midway between the Federal stronghold of Lexington and Frankfort, the state capital. It is also known as "the asparagus bed of the garden spot of Kentucky," whatever the hell that means.

We weren't after revenge for the Harrodsburg affair—or asparagus, for that matter—but we did want to stir up some of that old-fashioned terror that only a good guerrilla raid can inspire.

But mostly, we needed horses.

The flight from Bridgewater's column at Harrodsburg had taken its toll on the animals. Old Charley was limping along and favoring that front foot, but was still doing whatever I asked of him. Our aim was to steal enough fast horses so that we could outrun anything the Yankees had to offer; then, perhaps, I could leave Old Charley with a sympathetic farmer. Stealing horses was easy, but finding one I could trust was the hard part.

Mundy had already raided the town in November, and knew it was prime horse-stealing territory. During his earlier raid, Mundy had killed one man, Adam Harper, who had tried to prevent the horse theft—and the Federals had executed four rebel prisoners in retaliation. For this raid, we agreed not to kill anybody unless it became absolutely necessary.

We only had about thirty men, but we managed to raise a full complement of hell. The first thing we did was to wreck the telegraph office at the railway depot, so the operator would be unable to summon help. Then our revolvers persuaded the freight agent to open the safe, which we cleaned out, and after that we sloshed coal oil over the floors and set fire to the depot.

"What do we do if a train comes in filled with Yankees?" Mundy asked as he stood next to me and we admired the flames leaping from the roof and windows of the brick depot.

"We hold our ground," I said. "There's nothing more confused than a Yankee without orders. They are a dim-witted lot, devoid of spirit, and unusually docile in the face of a superior species."

"That has not been my experience," Mundy said.

He was a peculiar character and did resemble a girl, with his fine features and soft eyes and the hair brushing his shoulders. But there was nothing girlish about the way he stuck his revolver in the stomach of the first citizen we came to, a merchant who had rushed out of his mercantile store after seeing the smoke from the depot.

"Stand and deliver," Mundy said, "or digest lead."

The merchant rolled his eyes and dug in his pockets and produced a few coins and a handful of trade tokens. Mundy kept the coins, but tossed the tokens away, and asked if he had a pocket watch.

The merchant produced a battered watch and dangled it from its chain.

"To whom do I have the honor?" he asked.

Mundy snatched the watch and dropped it into his pocket.

"Sue Mundy, alias Captain Clark," he said. "And this is Captain Quantrill, formerly of Missouri. The trash you hand over now will become a treasure as the years pass. You will tell this story for your grandchildren, and they will sit upon your knees enthralled."

"You will both be long dead, I trust."

"You have some sand," Mundy remarked. "Aren't you afraid of getting shot?"

"Please," he said. "If you had my life, you'd be on your knees asking for a ball between the eyes."

"Well, what's so hard about your life?"

"You don't have enough time to hear the answer," he said. "But let's just say that if you were married to my wife, and had my brats, you would pray for death."

"I'll take your word for it," Mundy said. "Any money in that store of yours?"

"Nobody's had any cash money for a long while," he said. "The war. It's been strictly credit or barter for the last two years."

"Where are the best horses in the county?" I asked.

"Why should I tell you?" he asked.

"If you don't, I'm going to send a ball through that pumpkin-shaped head of yours," I said, cocking the Army and holding it against his temple. "And if you lie to us, we will ride back, burn your store to the ground, and then shoot you in the head."

"Best, how?" the merchant asked.

"The best blood," I said.

"The Alexander farm, just south of here," he said.

"What kind of horses?" I asked.

"Thoroughbreds, like you said. Robert Alexander breeds them to race."

"Now we're getting someplace," I said.

"But you'd best be careful," the merchant said. "Alexander has been expecting a raid ever since the news broke about you being in Kentucky, and he's taken precautions."

"What do you mean, precautions?" I asked.

"Don't know," the merchant said. "But he's not shy in talking about it—says if guerrillas want his horses, to let 'em come, because he's ready. I suppose that means he has the place under a heavy guard."

"Why would a farmer have such firepower at his command?"

"He's about as much of a farmer as the queen of England," he said. "He's rich, had some huge foundry operation along the Green River, but went bust and came back here to breed horses to race."

"What's his best horse?" I asked.

"Best, how—"

"Most famous," Mundy said. "Fastest. Won the most races."

"Oh, that would be the Airdrie Chief."

"Sounds like the one for me," Mundy said.

"Now," I told the merchant, "you understand that if you tell where we've gone . . ."

"Yes, yes," he said. "You'll come back and burn my store and put a pistol ball in my brain and probably kill my dog for good measure. Don't worry, I won't tell—the old man has been looking forward to somebody trying to steal his horses for a long time, and if I sent word to the cavalry, it would just spoil the experience for him."

"Good man," Mundy said.

As we walked away, I suggested that we find the local hotel and encourage the cook to fry us up some bacon and eggs and brew about a gallon of coffee to wash it down.

Mundy looked at me strangely.

"Bill," he said. "There is no time—you're not in Missouri anymore, where you could raid towns at your leisure. Here, we have to keep moving, or we're dead."

We rode in the front gate of Alexander's farm and right up to the big white house without encountering so much as a single shot—but we did see several hands drop their rifles and take off running across the fields.

Sue Mundy laughed.

Alexander himself was sitting on a rocker on the porch, smoking a pipe, looking quite serene except for the double-barreled shotgun across his lap. He calmly watched as we rode and dismounted.

"I'd appreciate it if you would hand that scattergun over, hammers down and butt-first," I said.

"No," Alexander said. "I might need it." He was fifty years old and spoke with a Scottish accent, and he adjusted the stem of the pipe and added, "I see that the hired help won't be requiring any more guns."

"We're here for your horses," Mundy said.

"I didn't think you were here for the conversation," Alexander said. "They're in the stable. You may have your pick, except for one."

"The Airdrie Chief?"

"Aye," he said. "That's why I need the shotgun."

"Well, walk with us down to the stable and we'll discuss it," I said.

He rose, tucked the shotgun beneath his arm, and led the way to the stable.

It was the finest stable I had ever seen, and far better than the houses most folks lived in. It was painted white with black trim and there were twenty-four stalls, and nearly every stall had a Thoroughbred in it.

"Where's the Chief?" Mundy asked.

"Over here," Alexander said, walking to the biggest stall.

Inside was the most beautiful horse I had ever seen—tall as Old Charley, but dark and built for speed. The stallion had a small head with a nice dished shape and bright, intelligent eyes.

"He's descended from the Darley Arabian," Alexander said. "The Darley was bought from the Bedouins in the Syrian desert for three hundred gold coins, but the sheikh changed his mind about parting with his favorite animal. But old Thomas Darley had some piratical friends and they stole the colt back and brought him to York in 1704. There is an unbroken line from that horse to the Airdrie Chief."

"What's Airdrie?"

"The town in Scotland where I was born," Alexander said.

"You can keep your horse," I said.

"Wait a minute," Mundy said.

"I said he can keep the horse," I repeated. "We can no more steal this horse than we could kidnap one of this old man's children. Take whatever else you want, there are plenty of fine horses to choose from."

"Dammit, Bill."

"No dammits about it," I said. "The Chief stays."

Alexander cleared his throat.

"You're a damned thief and you're about to ruin me by taking most of my stock," he said. "But since my hands have deserted me, I am at your mercy—and I thank you for this one great kindness."

We took nineteen horses—although I didn't find a replacement for Old Charley—and as we were riding away, Mundy told me what a damned fool I was.

"I know," I said.

* * *

A week later, we burned a wagon train near New Market, and the boys got out of hand—we killed seven Yankees. The telegraphs were kept busy clicking with the news, and it seemed like every Federal post in the state of Kentucky had dispatched troops to hunt us down.

One column chased us to Bradfordsville, in Marion County, where we decided to turn and fight. I formed the boys into a line, and when the Yankees saw we were getting ready, they dismounted and attempted to form their own line. But we charged before they could, and once we were upon then, we found that we had been cornered by a company of invalids.

Every one of them was missing an arm, or a leg, or an eye—once they had discharged their weapons, they couldn't hang on to their horses and reload their guns at the same time, so their line disintegrated.

We laughed and let them run.

Feeling fairly cocky, we returned to Hustonville, where we camped along the Little South Fork. But along about two o'clock in the morning, Bridgewater—who had done so much damage to John Barker and the boys at Harrodsburg—struck the camp and killed four of the boys and sent most of the rest of us scurrying into the snow-covered woods in our bare feet.

But I was able to mount Old Charley and escape.

The Yankees followed the footprints in the snow and killed three or four more of the boys. I had enough of fighting for a while, so I laid low for a while, but Sue Mundy didn't—he was cornered by some home guards in a tobacco barn near Webster, and spent a week nursing a wounded comrade. When the regular army came to get him, Mundy came out with guns blazing, wounding four of the Federals, but later surrendered under a flag of truce.

He was executed three days later at Louisville.

"I am a regular Confederate soldier and have served in the army for four years," he said, at least according to the newspapers. "I have taken many Federal soldiers prisoner and have always treated them kindly. I believe in and die for the Confederate cause."

Then they sent him through the trap, but the drop was only three feet. Instead of dying properly of a broken neck, Sue Mundy danced wildly while he was slowly strangled.

Blue Fugate

I was seduced by Kentucky.

With the coming of spring, the weather had turned warm and the hills had turned green with new grass. As the days passed, the hills became painted with dogwood and redbud, goldenrod and aster, and often I had the feeling that I was riding through a storybook landscape.

I could imagine no more idyllic setting than the Bluegrass country.

Because we had scattered after the execution of Sue Mundy, I found myself riding alone, or sometimes with Frank James or Doniphan Pence, avoiding the roads where the Yankees were apt to find me, and following instead the rivers and creeks, which ran clear and cold and supplied the water for the stills that were hidden in every hollow.

I was particularly fond of following the Salt River, and Simpson Creek and Ashes Creek, all of which were handy ways to reach several homesteads in Spencer and Nelson counties that offered refuge. The Salt River meanders through Taylorsville, while Simpson Creek runs through Bardstown and Ashes Creek runs to Bloomfield. Just about every farmhouse I encountered in the

backcountry acknowledged Southern sympathies. Few
eyebrows were raised as I introduced myself as Captain
Clarke of the Fourth Missouri *Confederate* Cavalry,
and when I mentioned some association with the Shepherd cousins, who were natives, or Donnie Pence, who
was from Missouri but had plenty of kin in Kentucky,
often the master of the house would break out a jug of
whiskey and toast Robert E. Lee until he could no
longer walk without risking bodily harm. Also, no matter how small the cabin or how poor the family, nearly
all of them had a name that was fit for an ancestral
estate.

I saw dogtrot cabins that I would be ashamed to call
home with names like *The Bourbon House* and *Eden on
Ashes Creek.* But near Bloomfield, there was the Dawson family's two-story cabin of chinked planks that was
named a little more honestly—it was called *Hungry
Run.*

Jim Dawson was a likable fellow and he had a
teenaged daughter named Nancy who seemed quite taken
with me. Early after we had arrived in Nelson County, I
had scratched out my cribbed Byron poem for her, and
from then on the Dawsons were newly found kin. It was
the same with John Russell and his daughter, Betty, on
Ashes Creek, and one day I presented her with the "My
Horse is at the Door" trash. Since, the Russells had been
pressing me for more visits, but truthfully I was not much
interested because Betty was a little older than the girls I
preferred. But I promised I would visit soon and take
breakfast.

At the village of Nazareth, northwest of Bardstown,
there was a girls academy run by the Sisters of Charity,
just one of a dozen or so Roman Catholic institutions that
dotted that county. South of Bardstown, there was a

monastery of Trappist monks that had fled France because of political unrest in 1848—and I wondered now whether they thought they had jumped out of the frying pan and into the fire. But the monks grew their own food and in doing so managed to survive the war. I sometimes visited the brown-robed monks, and was never refused a meal—usually of potatoes and milk—or denied a rope cot for the night.

Besides Catholics, the other thing Nelson County is lousy with is whiskey—and not just from the little still houses that one finds across the backcountry that dribble a few quarts a day into a stone jug, but large operations that produced several thousand barrels a year, at least before the war came. Now they were all shut down, except for a few men left to keep marauders from tearing the places apart board-by-board looking to scavenge a few drops.

There were half a dozen closed distilleries in the county, and when Donnie Pence and I first came upon one with its great warehouse where the barrels were stored, I asked Donnie why the warehouse and the trees and the fences were all painted black.

Pence laughed.

"Everybody asks that question at first," he said. "But it ain't paint. It's a kind of fungus that grows where whiskey is distilled or aged. Don't know what it's called, but it thrives on alcohol."

"I'll be damned," I said. "A guerrilla's paradise."

The stuff was so peculiar I had to dismount from Old Charley, walk over to one of the trees, and snap off a blackened twig. I tried to rub the stuff off with my thumb, but it was stubborn.

"There are a lot of barns about that are black," I said.

"I thought perhaps it was to help cure the tobacco crop, but is it this stuff?"

"Some of it, maybe," Pence said. "But a lot of that is actually paint. It's a tradition that goes back a long way, to the days when the government tried to tax the stills out of existence—when every barn and outbuilding on your place is painted black, it makes it hard to pick out the one where the still is."

Pence explained that Kentucky whiskey is not just any whiskey, either; it's bourbon whiskey, made from corn, and aged years in charred oak barrels. It was the honey-colored stuff the idiot Applewaith had given me during the last raid in Missouri, and while I had never been much of a drinker, I knew I could ruin myself on bourbon if given half a chance.

So I divided my time in Nelson County between visiting the Trappist monks for free meals and haunting the distilleries for the occasional bottle or jug the watchmen would slip me as an incentive to keep the boy from making trouble. Considering how well a distillery would burn, keeping me on their good side was only prudent.

I imagine they treated the Yankees the same.

During the communal meals at the monastery, I would often sit next to a monk named Guy—and that's pronounced "Ghee," because it's French—and he seemed to enjoy my company, though I was never sure. The monks had taken a vow of silence, and were allowed to speak only with their superiors when discussing religious business, and they communicated through hand gestures and animated glances.

I knew Brother Guy's name because I asked him, and had a pencil and a scrap of paper ready. He glanced around, guilty at first, and then jotted it down and smiled broadly.

After dinner one day, Guy accompanied me out to where Old Charley was hitched, and he was the perfect picture of peace—he walked slowly, with his arms clasped behind his back, and clear brown eyes that seemed to drink in the world.

"Are you happy?" I asked.

He nodded.

"I've killed men, you know," I said.

Again, he nodded.

"Not just a few men," I said. "A great number—hundreds, in fact. If I did not kill them personally, then they were killed at my direction. This is the way of war, I know, and while my numbers are a fraction of those accounted by Grant and Lee, I am called a monster."

He raised his eyebrows.

"Do you agree with them?"

He shrugged.

"It is not for you to judge, you're saying."

He nodded his agreement.

"Am I to have no peace?" I asked.

Brother Guy cleared his throat.

"I think I may be forgiven for breaking my silence," he said in a voice that was coarse from disuse and heavy with a French accent. "I cannot absolve you of your guilt. Only God can do that. As for peace—well, peace is where you find it. For me, it is here. For you, this place would be a prison. Find joy where you can, William Quantrill, but keep your heart open to the grace of God. It can come in some surprising ways."

I swung up onto Old Charley.

"Thank you for your kindness," I told Brother Guy. "And rest assured that you are under my protection. Should Yankees or anyone else interfere with the peace you have found here, I promise to fuck them up."

*   *   *

One April afternoon, after I had gotten my payoff from one of the distilleries and then gotten a hot meal with no conversation from the Trappists, I was walking Old Charley north along the bank of the Ashes Creek when I saw something flitting through the trees.

It looked like a girl—a blue girl.

I rubbed my eyes and looked again.

Nothing was moving except the leaves, which were shot with sunlight and gently swaying in the breeze. It was late in the afternoon, so I thought the movement must have been a squirrel, dashing from one tree to another, hiding behind a tree trunk when I stopped to look.

"Well," I said, patting Old Charley's neck, "it's time to find a place to sleep it off when you start thinking squirrels are blue women running through the woods."

I nudged Old Charley forward, and we followed the path until it crossed the creek at a ford, and in the middle I stopped and allowed my horse to take some water.

Then I saw a face staring at me over the top of a log, thirty yards away.

I drew the Army and slipped down from the saddle, my boot splashing in the water. Then I waded down the creek to where I had seen the face, my revolver held at the ready.

"Who's there?" I asked.

I was within ten feet of the log, but there was no answer.

"I know you're there," I said. "Tell me why you're spying on me. You'd best answer, or I will assume you mean me harm and will proceed accordingly."

I cocked the revolver.

A pair of small hands appeared above the log.

The hands were *blue*.

"Don't shoot," a soft voice said.

"Show yourself."

Slowly, a girl fourteen or perhaps fifteen stood. She was thin, had straight red hair that fell to the middle of her back, and wore a dirty muslin dress. The sun was shining behind her, and I could tell that she was wearing nothing beneath the dress. But the most remarkable thing was that her skin had a decidedly blue cast, similar to the color of a robin's egg, and her lips were positively purple.

"What's wrong with you?"

"Nothin'," the girl said.

"You are not ill?" I asked.

"Nope," she said.

"Have you been dyeing clothes, or stained yourself with berries, or otherwise painted yourself?"

"No, dammit," she said. "It's a natural condition. My name is Hyacinth Fugate, but most folks just call me Blue. I'm of the original Fugate stock of Troublesome Creek, in the mountains east of here, and most of us look this way. It gets worse when we're agitated, and I can guarantee you that I'm damned well agitated now."

Her accent told me she wasn't lying about where she called home.

"Well, your nickname suits you well—you cuss a blue streak," I said, uncocking the revolver. "What are you doing here?"

"Running away," she said.

"Why?"

Her eyes widened, as if shocked that anyone wouldn't understand. "You've never heard of Troublesome Creek, have you?"

"No, Blue," I said. "I'm from Missouri."

"Well, there is not much to do on Troublesome Creek except scramble for a living," she said. "The Fugates marry the living hell out of each other, and I'm promised to my cousin Isaiah, who is as blue as I am."

"You don't care for him."

"No, sir," she said. "I hate his fucking guts, and I'll be damned if I'm going to raise a brood of blue brats. So I lit out, figuring I could shift for myself better than my family ever did, and look for somebody who didn't make me want to puke every time I got a whiff of him and maybe even give me some pink babies."

During the speech, the strap of her dress had fallen off her left shoulder, revealing a breast that was surprisingly full for such a thin girl.

"You're undressed," I said.

"Shit," she said. "That ain't nothing."

She smiled and took her time about tugging the strap back up.

"Who taught you to cuss?" I asked.

"What do you mean?"

"Your language," I said. "It's as coarse as anything I've heard from men."

"You should hear my ma," she said, rolling her eyes. "When she gets mad, she can rip off a string that will part your hair, curdle milk, and peel the paint right off the walls. Why, does it bother you?"

"Not really," I said. "But I would advise you to watch your language around women. Other women, I mean."

"Thank you," she said. "I will heed the advice."

"Blue, why were you following me?"

"Oh, I've been watching you for the last week or so," she said, doing her best to flirt. "I've taken up residence in that abandoned cabin yonder, and from there I can see

you and your big white horse riding down Ashes Creek
and then coming back a few hours later. You are a guerrilla and I reckon you are the man to know."

"Why?"

"Look at me," she said, holding out her hands. "I'm
goddamned starving to death! Also, you're really *pink*."

Ashes Creek

The cabin in which Blue Fugate was squatting proved a horror, but I didn't care. I dropped Old Charley's reins on the ground and swept Blue up in my arms, kicked the flimsy door from its hinges, carried her over the threshold, kissed her deeply and looked around for a clean spot to deposit her and, finding none, placed her on the wooden table beneath a broken window.

"What do you want?" she asked, hands reaching for my belt as red hair fell in her face. She shook her head and pursed her lips and blew the hair out of her eyes as her fingers unhooked the buckle. "I can do anything, anything at all. I don't mind. This is a good time, because I ain't bleeding yet. Just don't hit me, unless that's what busts your cap. It isn't, is it?"

"No," I said, "I don't strike women."

My left hand was behind her neck and the other was sliding between her thighs. Her eyes were hard and mischievous and her breasts swelled against the fabric of her dress as her breathing became deeper and she wet her dark lips with her tongue. I was surprised by how much I wanted this girl; under other circumstances, I wouldn't have given her a second glance. Granted, I was lonely, but there was something else—the girl was uneducated, of course, but had a quick animal intelligence and an absolute lack of shame or self-consciousness that appealed to me. Girls lose that by sixteen or so. Whatever happened, there would be no regrets or apologies, no recriminations or claims of betrayal. In age and demeanor she reminded me of Kate King, a girl I had spent some weeks with back in Missouri, and the thought made me press against her a bit harder.

"Wait," she said, placing her hands against my chest. She pushed me back a bit, then drew her legs beneath her and crouched on the table. Crossing her arms, she gathered a handful of muslin in each hand and pulled the dress over her head. She was thin, but her breasts were disappointingly fuller than I expected, and her nipples were as blue as her lips. The skin across her throat and breasts was a mottled pink. Her ribs were like gills on either side of her chest.

"There," she said, tossing the dress aside. "That's better, ain't it?"

She seemed a creature from a storybook. With my fingertips I brushed her hair behind her left ear, half expecting the tip of that ear to be pointed. Her head jerked a bit, as if she expected something rougher.

"Now you," she said, and began to unbutton my shirt.

I pulled the Army from my waist and hung it from the trigger guard on a rusty nail next to the broken window.

"Damn, but you have a lot of clothes," she complained. "It's spring. What do you need all of this stuff for? Oh, I like this sash. Can I wear it?" She looped the wine-colored cloth a couple of times around her neck and let the tassels hang between her breasts. She knelt on one knee, then continued to divest me of my clothing. "Damn, this is heavy. What the hell is in your pockets?"

"Powder," I said. "Balls. Percussion caps."

"Where're you from?"

"Missouri."

"Born there?"

"No. Ohio."

"Across the river."

"Three hundred miles across the river."

"Yankees?"

"Yes, my family are Yankees all."

"Your people," she said. "Are they like you? I mean, are they all so damned white? Blond and blue-eyed? Good. Most born healthy, I reckon?"

"Mostly."

"No cripples?"

I didn't mention my sister, Mary.

"What'd you do before the war?"

"Schoolteacher," I said. "Thief."

"No shame in that," she said. "Hell, if it wasn't for stealing, I would have starved and gone to hell." She motioned for my boots. "How many men you killed?"

"Personally or had killed? A dozen, personally. Hundreds, on my order."

She paused, my left boot in her lap. She cocked her head to one side and grinned. "You're full of shit."

"Often," I said. "But not about this. Have you heard of Lawrence, Kansas?"

"Heard of Kansas," she said. "You some kind of general or something?"

"Or something," I said.

"You some kind of big casino?"

"A captain," I said. "I was once a brevet colonel, but not being one to stand on formality, I discourage the men from referring to me as colonel. It would be an empty title."

"I didn't understand one damned word you just said," she said. "Tell me plain, how many soldiers do you get to boss about?"

I said I commanded thirty or forty partisans, scattered across Nelson and Spencer counties. That we were hiding now because the Yankees would shoot us on sight, but that we would regroup soon and keep moving.

"So you're headed home," she said. "Across the river."

"I don't feel like talking just now," I said, tugging off the remaining boot. "You talk more than any three girls, and cuss more than most men. Would you shut up and let me get down to business?"

"You want to fucking hit me?" she asked. "You can, if you want. Do it now. Just use the flat of your hand, not your fist. Slap me a bit, just don't draw any blood, because I don't like that—"

"I'm not going to hit you, Blue."

She chewed her lower lip.

"All men hit," she said. "They say they don't, but they do. It's best to get it over with right away. If you hit me hard now, you can be sorry and promise to never do it again and explain to me as how you had to do it because you love me so."

"I don't love you," I said. "And I'm not going to hit you."

"Right," she said. "That makes sense."

She ran her hands over my chest and stomach.

"When's your birthday?" she asked. "The year, I mean. I reckon you're old, maybe thirty, but I could be wrong. It's hard to tell with some people. With you, I reckon you act older than you really are. This is a gunshot wound here, ain't it? How'd you get—"

I put my hand over her mouth.

Her eyes grew wide.

"Ten minutes," I said. "Just give me ten minutes with no questions. In fact, no talking at all. Agreed?"

This is more than you want to know about Blue Fugate, and I've already spoken more frankly than I should have—and yet, I need to finish this part of my story. Because I have no one else in whom I can confide, and because you are no doubt familiar with marital relations, I ask you to endure the rest.

Our union is fierce.

She sits unashamedly, her knees drawn up and her dirty feet on the dusty tabletop, and the wine-colored tassels hang between her breasts. She draws me into her and then presses tightly against me, her face nuzzling the three-day stubble on my cheeks, her right hand clutching a fistful of my hair just above the back of my neck. I stare past her shoulder and through a broken windowpane to the scene beyond, and it seems as if I am gazing into a painting. Old Charley is a white horse against a green hillside, tree branches sway in the breeze, the sun glints from Ashes Creek.

The moment lasts forever.

Then the quickening comes as Old Charley dips his head and tears at some shrubbery beneath the porch, searching for something tender. A sound is building in Blue's throat, a strange keening, and her body shudders. The keen turns into a scream, and there is a fierce cracking sound as the table beneath her goes to pieces and drops away, but she does not fall because she is climbing me like a tree. I reach my zenith and stay there for some unbearable seconds. My left arm is behind the small of Blue's back, but my right arm is free, and I make a fist and shatter one of the unbroken panes of window glass.

"Bingo," Blue exclaims.

Old Charley has pulled the shrub completely free of

the earth and is breaking it apart and I am fascinated by the act of his mastication—the muscles rippling along his massive jawbone, the great yellow teeth, the elastic and quivering muzzle.

"It is a bawdy world," I say.

"Shit, you're bleeding."

Blood is running from the back of my hand over my wrist and dripping from my forearm onto Blue's chest and stomach. The blood seems bright, brighter than I ever remember it being. But then my mind flashes on Jim Little, his hair matted with blood, and the blood that was dripping on the floor of the cabin after he put the pistol ball through his brain was just as bright.

That ball is now seated in the first chamber of the Army.

I reach for the revolver, which hangs on the nail beside the window, but Blue catches my arm in both hands before my fingers can close on the grips. Then Blue removes the sash from her neck and wraps it around my bleeding hand.

"It'll stain." I jerk my hand away.

"It's the same damn color, you won't be able to tell it," she says, jerking it back. "Besides, it's the only thing we have for a bandage. Men. What the fuck is wrong with all of you? No, you don't hit women, but you will put your hand through a pane of glass. And why the hell were you reaching for the gun after?"

I don't answer.

"Were you going to shoot you or shoot me?"

"I wasn't going to shoot you."

"Christ on a stick," she says. "You didn't tell me that madness runs in your family. That's a bit of a deal breaker, but I suppose it might be too late to worry about now."

"I'm not insane. The impulse has passed."

"Good."

She smiles wickedly. She lifts my arm and, with her tongue, laps up a rivulet of blood running toward my elbow. She licks her lips, then uses the back of her hand to wipe her mouth.

April 13

The next day, I came back with a few of the boys who could swing a hammer. They fixed the door and patched the window and made the cabin almost suitable for human habitation. Then I passed the word among our friends in the county to keep an eye on the girl on Ashes Creek, and little gifts began to show up on the cabin's porch—a dress, a pitcher of buttermilk, a basket of food.

A Bible or two was left, but they were of little use to Blue.

She asked me to read her some of it, but she stopped me before I got through the second chapter of Genesis. She asked me to read instead the Louisville paper, so I withdrew a paper that was only a week old and began to read her the news of how Lee had surrendered at Appomattox Courthouse in Virginia.

"Not that part."

"Do you not care that the end of the war is at hand?"

"I'd rather hear about the things to buy."

So I picked an advertisement at random and informed her of the Metallic Artificial Legs made of corrugated brass by the Universal Joint and Artificial Limb Company. Offered by Mr. J. W. Weston on Market Street.

Prices, eighty dollars for civilians, fifty dollars for soldiers.

"Eighty dollars! Nobody has that much money."

"Some do. And if they are in need of a limb, they will spend it."

"More."

Next was laundry soap, followed by hair curlers and Farnham's permanent cure of asthma, which guaranteed relief in five minutes. In an adjacent column, Dr. Baxter on Magazine Street offered a foolproof cure for drunkenness and opium eating.

"People buy these things and they work?"

"They buy them," I said. "Sometimes they work."

"Which ones don't work?"

"The worse you want or need something to work, the poorer the chances. If you want to be freed of asthma or an addiction to opium, the odds are slim indeed. But if you want clean clothes or curly hair, you'll likely get it."

"And these people who sell the things that don't work, how do they keep on selling? Don't the people that are disappointed come around in the middle of the night and knock them on the head and take their money back?"

"No, that would be a crime."

"But it ain't to cheat people."

"It's called business."

"But why don't these cheats go out of business right quick?"

"Because there are so many people in Louisville that they couldn't cheat all of them in a single lifetime, so there is always somebody new to fool."

"So, how many folks live in Louisville?"

"Sixty or seventy thousand."

"You're full of shit," she said.

"You must find another favorite expression of surprise.

And no, I am not teasing you—there really are that many people in Louisville, and probably more, if you count the soldiers passing through."

"There ain't fifty people back home on Troublesome Creek," she said. "Seventy thousand! With their pockets stuffed with money, and clean clothes, and curly hair, and some of them walking around on corrugated brass legs."

"A few, I suppose."

"Someday," she said, "I want to visit Louisville."

"You will. I'm sure of it."

I added the shack to my rounds in Nelson County, alternating fairly regular between there and Wakefield Farm, just north of the line into Spencer County. The farm was owned by Old Jim Wakefield, a Southern sympathizer who could always be counted on to produce a jug of bourbon whiskey or two.

Meanwhile, the Yankees kept arresting the associates of poor dead Sue Mundy, including a pair named Metcalf and Magruder. Then a guerrilla named Billy Marion kidnapped a Federal surgeon and threatened to kill him unless the pair was released. The Yankees were singularly unimpressed, and General Palmer replied in the newspapers that Metcalf and Magruder would be immediately hanged if any harm came to the doctor.

On the thirteenth of April, I chanced upon Billy Marion in Bloomfield, a few miles south of Wakefield Farm. He was on his back in the middle of the street, drunk. Marion was large, but quite fat, and his stomach made a hump like a buffalo's. Beside him was a bottle of whiskey. His horse was dragging its reins on the ground, thirty yards away.

"Where's your surgeon?"

"Gone."

Marion was staring skyward. At the apex of his great round stomach was a Federal military issue brass buckle with the letters U.S. emblazoned upon it—but Marion wore it upside down, as many Rebels did with captured buckles. Hanging from a cord around his neck was a Lefaucheux revolver.

"You killed him?"

"Escaped," Marion said.

"How'd that happen?"

Marion held up the bottle. "I began drinking again yesterday."

He struggled to sit up, but could not.

I had a dozen of the boys with me, and a couple of them jumped down from their horses and helped Marion to his feet. Another went to fetch his horse, but the animal kept moving just far enough away to keep the reins beyond his grasp.

"You're a disgrace," I said.

"Thank you."

I swung down from the saddle. He offered me the bottle, which was nearly empty, and I tipped it back and allowed the last of the bourbon to slide down my throat.

"How'd you know about the surgeon?"

He reached out to pat Old Charley, but the horse snapped and he withdrew his hand just in time to save his fingers. "Read it in the papers. Where's the men?"

"In there," he said, throwing an arm behind him to indicate a brick storefront that housed a well-known brothel on the second floor. "I have lost my surgeon and we have lost the war. My desire has become a pathetic and despised thing, so it seemed best that I stay in the road and drink."

"I understand now," I said. "May I see that piece that swings beneath from your neck?"

"Ah, the French revolver." He unsnapped the clip that attached the lanyard to the swivel at the heel of the gun, then offered it to me butt-first. It was .44 caliber, the same as my Colt's Army, but it was lighter and a few inches shorter. But the grips were even bigger than the Army, which put most of the mass of the revolver in your palm, and aiming it seemed like pointing one's finger.

"The French are a clever and warlike people," I said. "How do you get rounds for it?"

The Lefaucheux used pin-fire cartridges that had to be imported from France, and with the blockade there was virtually no chance of any ammunition making it into the South. And while the revolvers weren't exactly rare among Yankee troops, they were uncommon, so the chances of capturing additional rounds was unlikely.

"I don't. Captured it from a Yankee trooper over near Bardstown. Figured if it was good enough for Stonewall Jackson to be presented with a Lefaucheux by his troops, it was good enough for me. So I only have six rounds."

"Damn lawyers," I said.

Even though American arms manufacturers had perfected revolvers that took internally primed ammunition, a lawsuit declaring patent infringement had prevented any cartridge sidearms from reaching production. But this injunction had placed no restraints on the importation of foreign sidearms, and a few found their way into the hands of both armies.

"Why do you keep it on a string around your neck?"

"It is a weapon of last resort. Also, I am frequently drunk and misplace my other pistols."

"Forward thinking."

Marion slapped me on the back so hard that I stumbled forward.

"Let's visit the girls on the second floor," he suggested. "I think the redheaded one with the round bottom might coax my desire to flame anew."

I said no, but Marion began to pull me toward the building.

At that moment, there was a clatter of hooves at the far end of the street. A company of riders raced toward us, and I saw the glint of sunlight on metal as carbines were unlimbered. But the most remarkable thing about this squad of riders is that they were dressed in high-collared red jackets and baggy pants.

At first I thought they were Zouaves, whose uniforms were patterned after those worn by Turkish troops fighting for the French in Algiers. Even before the war, Zouaves were all the rage, and red-jacketed drill teams were popular across the country. Even though the slaughter of the last few years had disabused most Americans of their romantic notions of war, the fez-wearing or turbaned Zouave units remained inexplicably popular.

"Zouaves?"

"Hell, no," Marion said, and spat. "That's Terrell, the guerrilla hunter. We'd best be moving, because those carbines they are preparing to use against us are Spencers."

Spencers are lever-action repeaters and hold seven rounds in a tubular magazine in the stock and one in the chamber, allowing a trooper to fire eight times before reloading. The legal trouble that kept cartridge revolvers off the American market did not apply to long guns; while the Federals had been slow to adopt repeaters, we had been seeing more Spencers and even Henrys in Yankee hands in the past year.

The carbines began to boom, and I could hear the .52-caliber slugs zinging past and slapping the bricks just behind me. Suddenly sober, Marion took the Lefaucheux from my grasp, cocked it, and aimed offhanded at the lead rider. The pistol barked. The rider fell into the street, still clutching the carbine. He made a motion to lever another round into the chamber, and then was still.

"Ha!" Marion roared. "You are kilt with a French pistol."

I pulled the Army from my sash and cocked it, then lowered the hammer with my thumb, and cocked it again, so as to ratchet the cylinder past the ball that had ended the life of Jim Little. I would use it, if I had to, but I wouldn't waste it as my first shot. Then I planted my feet, pressed my clenched left fist to the small of my back, and took offhand aim at a red-jacketed corporal. I squeezed the trigger just as he was bringing his carbine to bear upon me, and the Army spat lead and smoke. Then I cocked the gun and took aim at the next trooper and fired, then thumbed the hammer back again and looked for another target through the smoke.

Having four of their number shot from the saddle had halted the Yankees' charge a hundred yards down the street. There was a lot of smoke between us, but I could catch glimpses of them turning and cutting their horses, trying to reform, while a small man with a brutish face and dark, untamed hair screamed at them.

Marion laughed like an idiot.

"You're damned good," he said.

"I've had some practice. Who's the monkeylike fellow?"

"That's Ed Terrell himself," Marion said. "He's been asking around the county about you—wants to know if anybody has seen you and, if they have, to tell him in detail what you look like. So far, he hasn't found anybody who will admit to getting a good enough look to describe you."

Impulsively, he picked up the empty whiskey bottle

and pitched it in a running throw down the street. It sailed in a tumbling shallow arc, rose above the smoke, and glittered in the sun, then plunged down and shattered on the bricks a few dozen yards from Terrell.

"I fucked your sister last night, Edwin!" Marion shouted. "She said I was better than you, but not as good as your old man!"

I made a clucking sound and Old Charley walked over to me and offered his left side just as calm and surefooted as if there had been no trouble at all in the street. I put my boot into the stirrup and swung up into the saddle.

Marion's crew was pouring out of the door that led to the whorehouse, some of them in their underwear, but all with a pistol or rifle in their hands.

Things had happened so quickly that most of my boys hadn't fired a shot. Many of them were quite green, were left without a leader after Sue Mundy was executed, and I doubt that any of them had fired a full cylinder in anger.

Frank James, however, had a smoking Remington in his hand.

"Who the hell is that?" he asked from the saddle. "If they're trying to look like Zouaves, they've missed by a far piece. They look like circus performers in those little red suits."

"Those are the Yankee guerrilla hunters sent to kill us," I said.

"Well, they've got the iron to do the job, if not the smarts," he said.

"Damn Spencers," I said. "If they manage to regroup, they'll cut right through us."

"Then we make a run for it."

"Not yet," I said. "We're going to make a run to scatter them one last time, so that Billy and his boys can mount up. After we break through, we keep right on going—while Marion goes in the other direction."

"Fair enough," Frank said, then shouted for the boys to form their horses in a line damned quick. Marion had found his horse now, and was climbing into the saddle.

When our boys were more or less formed up, Frank nodded.

"If you get a chance," I told him, "kill the little sonuvabitch with the captain's stripes."

"Love to."

I touched my spurs to Old Charley's flanks and he bolted forward, and Frank and some of the new boys followed. A few went the other direction. We closed the distance between us and the guerrilla hunters in ten or twenty seconds, our pistols popping as we rode. A couple of the troopers managed to shoulder their carbines and get a few shots off, and I heard one of my boys fall to the ground behind me.

By the time we reached them, Old Charley was in full gallop—his hooves were drumming groups of four beats on the bricks, and floating between groups. And then we plowed into the group, and the sheer momentum of Charley's twelve hundred pounds bowled one of the Yankees' horses over and spilled its rider on the ground. He abandoned his Spencer and scrambled away to keep from being trampled to death; then I jerked Old Charley's reins to the left and dug my left spur into his flank, making him wheel hard and allowing the maximum sweep for the Army in my right hand. I was looking for the small man that Marion had identified as Terrell, but in the confusion did not see him.

"Where is he?" I shouted at Frank.

Frank shook his head.

"Goddammit," I said. "We have not time."

Then I saw Terrell through the black powder smoke.
His horse had been shot from under him and he had hit
the street hard. He was struggling to get out from beneath
the animal, and he must have landed on his left shoulder,
because he was favoring it in a peculiar way. But his right
hand kept the Spencer in a tight grip.

Frank threw the Remington down on him and pulled
the trigger, but the percussion cap gave a pitiful little
pop!—a misfire. Then he shouted to me that he had shot
all of his pistols dry.

I tried to aim the Army at Terrell, but a couple of my
own men rode unwittingly in between. I spurred Old
Charley forward and cut hard around them, and was lev-
eling the Remington when I was suddenly pitched forward and the shot—the Jim Little ball—went wild and
punched a hole in the paving brick. There was so much
noise and action, however, that Terrell hadn't even looked
up—and did not know he had escaped death by the
slimmest of margins.

I had been thrown over Old Charley's neck into the
street. It was the only time he ever fell with me, and it left
me on foot in the midst of a mounted battle with an empty
pistol. One of the new recruits raced over and reached
down to pull me into the saddle, and as our hands met his
head was furrowed by a Spencer ball.

He fell dead at my feet.

I never learned his name.

I stepped over the body and grabbed the reins of the
dead boy's horse, then got a boot into the stirrup and
climbed up into the saddle. Old Charley had rolled back
on his feet, and was limping aimlessly about.

"Let's go," Frank shouted.

"I can't leave him."

"The boy's dead."

"Old Charley," I said.

"Stay here and you'll die," Frank said.

As we tore out of town toward Taylorsville, Marion and his crew provided covering fire. When Terrell and his men finally got formed up, all of them rode south, chasing Billy Marion. Then I went back into town and put a lead on Old Charley.

The Coffin Bone

We rode to Jim Wakefield's farm.

The blacksmith back in Christian County had been right—the strain of hard riding had been too much for Old Charley. One of the boys, Jack Graham, had been a ferrier before the war, and offered to see what he could do. He borrowed some tools from old Wakefield, removed the special shoe, and tried to pare the hoof with a buttress, a chisel-like device that is about a foot long, in such a way that it would ease the strain. I was hanging on to Charley's bridle, trying to calm him, because he hated anybody but me near him. But Old Charley jerked his head loose and nipped Graham, who yelped and clutched his bleeding hand.

"It's no use, Captain," Graham said. "He's lame. I'm sorry."

"It's not your fault," I said, patting Old Charley's neck.

"You know what you have to do," Frank said.

I didn't respond.

"Let me do it, then."

"I'll do it."

I unsaddled Old Charley and then walked him out of the lot and down to the pond, where I let him drink his fill. It was a pleasant April afternoon. There was a mild breeze from the south. On the pond, a couple of farm ducks were paddling lazily about.

Old Charley lifted his head, his muzzle dripping with water, and he regarded me with a soft black eye. I ran my hand over his hide, pausing at the puckered places where he had taken a gunshot.

Then I pressed the muzzle against his skull, just over his left eye.

"Farewell, cousin."

I pulled the trigger. Old Charley fell heavily at the water's edge, scattering the ducks. I sat down next to him and cried for a quarter of an hour. Then I walked back to the lot and told the boys to get rid of the carcass in any way that old Wakefield wanted, but that I didn't want to know about it.

"Captain, I know your heart is broken," Frank said. "But you'll find another good horse, in time."

"No, my work is done."

"Don't talk so."

"Death is coming," I said.

Two days later, Billy Marion was ambushed at a still house near Bloomfield by a company of state guards. He was shot while attempting to mount his horse. The state guards left Marion where he fell while they chased the four guerrillas who had been drinking with Marion.

Not long after, Edwin Terrell arrived at the still house and found Marion's body on the ground. He slung the corpse across a saddle, carried it to the depot at Bardstown, and took it by rail to Louisville. There, Terrell lugged the body to General Palmer's headquarters and claimed that he had killed Billy Marion—and, according to the papers, had rescued the kidnapped surgeon.

The day before Marion was killed, Abraham Lincoln was assassinated.

When we heard the news, the boys and I got famously drunk at Old Jim Wakefield's place. There were many toasts, to the memory of Billy Marion and other fallen comrades, and to the notion that Abraham Lincoln was now roasting in hell. But even though I drank plenty of bourbon, I could take no pleasure in the passing of the archfiend.

Now that Lee had surrendered the Army of Northern Virginia, and the actor John Wilkes Booth had settled the score with Lincoln, there was little left for me to do—except to go home.

Still, I lingered.

A Hard Rain

Now we come to the second thing the foolish always ask about, and that is the affair at Wakefield Farm. The time has come at last to describe it in some detail. There isn't much more to tell once we are done with this, and while it might seem strange to say, I'm glad of it; there's nothing as hard to accomplish as an honest recollection, and I am tired to death of doing it.

It was a Wednesday morning, the tenth of May.

I had spent the night at Blue Fugate's shack, with twenty of the fellows standing guard. They were Kentucky boys, mostly, with a few of the Missouri old-timers thrown in for good measure. Frank James, however, was away somewhere, feeding his belly or his purse.

I left the shack before dawn, and already there was the feeling of a coming storm. Lightning flashed in the west and distant thunder rolled over the hills. Blue Fugate lingered in the doorway as I mounted my horse. She leaned against the door frame, her dark hair spilling over her shoulders, and the breeze rippling her nightclothes. By prior agreement, we did not exchange waves or say goodbyes. To do so would make every parting seem the last;

also, when I was finally gone, I wanted her to be unaware the blow was coming.

"A hard rain is coming," she said as I swung up into the saddle.

"It appears so," I said, glancing at the sky.

Then I rode away without looking back.

Even though I was fagged out, I remembered my promise to John Russell and took the boys to his cabin on Ashes Creek. We had breakfast there and after, Russell's daughter, Betty, gave me a horse. She made a show of presenting it, and I felt obliged to accept the gift, even though I was uninterested in the girl because she was nearing twenty and did not want the animal because it was a saddle horse that had never been subjected to gunfire and was unused to the rough treatment required in battle. The horse's name was Blackie, which I also disliked, because that's the name given by silly girls to every other horse with a dark coat. But I dutifully slipped my bridle and saddle on the animal and rode him north on the Bloomfield-Taylorsville Road. One of the boys slipped a rope around the halter of the horse I had been riding and allowed him to trail behind.

Rather than pleasing me, the gift horse just made me think about the passing of Old Charley and increased my melancholy. I was also fatigued from the heavy drinking and a lack of sleep, and my fondest wish was simply to stretch out in the loft of Wakefield's and nap for a few hours.

It was only a few miles from Ashes Creek to the big gate that marked the lane to the Wakefield Farm, and the dark storm clouds were fairly touching the tops of the rolling hills. We reached the gate at about ten o'clock, and I noted that Almstead Jacobs, the freedman blacksmith whom I had questioned about Salt River, was at his forge.

He watched us pass, and I nodded in his direction, but he did not raise a hand in greeting or give any other sign of recogntion.

"To hell with him," I muttered.

We crested the top of the hill, where we could see the Wakefield house and the barn and the yard, and I was relieved to see that nothing seemed out of the ordinary. Old Jim Wakefield was sitting on his porch and he waved as we rode into the lot. Before we reached the barn, however, it began to rain buckets and we were all soaked as we dismounted and threw the reins around the rack in the yard. If it hadn't been raining, I would have taken the time to throw my saddle on my former mount, but was so tired that I decided it could wait until things dried up a bit.

I climbed up the ladder to the hayloft, shucked my outer clothes, pulled off my boots, and stretched out. Sleep should have been as easy as rolling off a log, considering how tired I was and my relative comfort and the sound of the cool rain drumming on the roof of the barn. But I could not still my mind. I began thinking about home and the letter I had been trying to write for five years. The task seemed as impossible as assaulting that blockhouse at Fayette. It would take volumes to explain what had happened to me since my last letter from Kansas Territory, and my fulsome praise of the abolitionists. How to explain my conversion to the Southern cause and my belief that slavery was God's natural law, as evidenced in the Bible? How to describe my transformation from a ne'er-do-well and petty thief into a cavalry strategist and leader of desperate men whose name inspired terror in the hearts of his enemies? And then there was Lawrence.

To hell with it, I thought.

Best to appear unannounced on my mother's doorstep. I imagined the smile on my sister Mary's face and a tearful reunion with my mother, and how she would beg forgiveness for how meanly she had treated me as a child. She would marvel at how I had placed the family name on the lips of every newspaper reader in America. And she would tell me how pleased my father would be if he could see that I had become a man to be reckoned with.

I would slip out soon, I decided—that very night, or the next, or perhaps I would stay longer and reprovision my purse through another raid or two. In any case, I wouldn't tarry much longer in Kentucky, as home was just a fortnight of easy riding away. I would leave the boys and my old clothes behind and would assume a new identity.

Then it stopped raining and I could hear the boys talking and laughing below. I could also hear the rough voice of Old Wakefield, who had brought over a jug of whiskey and was sharing it with Dick Glasscock beneath the shed near the barn. Then one of the boys started a corncob war with another, and soon the others had joined in, and they were running and pelting one another with cobs and generally behaving like a bunch of schoolboys at recess.

Then I heard Clark Hockensmith cry out, "Here they come!"

This was immediately followed by the sound of carbine fire and pistol shots mixing.

I snatched up my trousers and pulled them on, followed by my boots. I pushed the Army into my belt. I hadn't heard the sound of the Yankee horses because the ground was wet and the boys were making too much noise with their corncob fight. Leaving my jacket behind, I flew down the ladder and, with my Army in my hand, ran out into the barnyard, which was a perfect scene of chaos.

Thirty or forty riders clad in shell jackets were pouring down the hill toward us, their long guns barking. Some of the boys were running off on foot to the north, but most were dashing for their horses. William Noland, however, was standing in the middle of the yard, a pistol in each hand. He had not yet raised his guns.

"Come on, damn you!" he taunted.

The lead rider bore down, leveled his carbine, and shot Noland in the chest before he could fire either of the pistols. Then the rider trampled Noland beneath the hooves of the horse.

By the time I reached the hitching rack, Blackie was the only horse left.

I slipped the reins and tried to mount, but the horse was rearing and bucking and attempting to get away. The lot was slick with mud and I stumbled and slid as I attempted to get control of the horse. Then I got my left boot up into the stirrup and grasped the edge of the saddle, but when I attempted to throw myself up into the saddle, Blackie rose on two legs and threw me off.

"Damn you," I cursed while I sat in the mud and the horse trotted away to the north. I sprang up and began running down the bridle path to the south, toward an apple orchard. Glasscock and Hockensmith were about to jump their horses over the fence into the orchard when they heard me call out.

"Boys!" I called. "Help me!"

They wheeled their horses and came riding back for me, firing their pistols to slow the advance of Terrell and his men. I reached Glasscock first, and he bared his cannibal teeth as he fired calmly at the approaching redcoats.

He offered me his left hand and I pulled myself up into the saddle behind him, but then one of those Spencer repeaters boomed and the ball struck the horse in the hip. The animal screamed—and if you don't think a horse can scream you've never seen battle—then it wheeled and sank, spilling both of us onto the bridle path.

Glasscock got up and started running for all he was worth toward the orchard fence. I fired twice with the Army as I got to my feet, then sprinted for Clark Hockensmith, who still had a horse under him. Hockensmith slowed his horse and tried to pull me up beside him when I heard one of the damned Spencers bark again.

Suddenly I was facedown in the mud.

The shot must have missed me and struck Hockensmith's horse in the flank, I thought, and then the horse must have kicked the daylights out of me. Stars swirled and reeled before my eyes. The wind had been knocked out of me, and I lay there for a moment gasping for breath like a fish that has been pulled from the water.

I pushed myself up with my left arm. My revolver lay in the mud a couple of feet away. We were still only halfway down the bridle path toward the orchard, although Hockensmith was making a desperate ride for the fence. Then from behind I heard another carbine shot boom and Hockensmith was knocked out of the saddle. I could tell by the way he rolled, like so much laundry, that he was dead before his body hit the ground. His horse stopped running and came back to stand near the body, its reins trailing on the ground.

Glasscock, who was still scrambling about on foot, lunged for the animal. At that moment a Yankee guerrilla thundered past me, his horse flinging great clods of mud, and he held the reins in his left hand as he brought the carbine to his cheek with his right. Glasscock had apparently shot his pistols dry, as both of his hands were empty.

I reached for the Army with my right hand.

Another redcoat rode past and snapped off a pistol shot in my direction. The ball severed the trigger finger of my right hand as cleanly as if a surgeon had done it, although I did not realize it until after I had grasped and cocked the Army and thought I was pulling the trigger but was puzzled because nothing was happening.

Then the two Yankee guerrillas leisurely shot Glasscock to death.

The one with the Spencer fired first, and the ball hit him in the shoulder and spun him around, but Dick remained on his feet. Then the one with the Starr revolver extended his hand and pulled the trigger, and Glasscock took the shot squarely in the middle of his forehead. He dropped to his knees, then fell face-first into the muddy path.

My right hand felt like warm water was being poured over it, but that was the blood gushing from the stump of my index finger. I aimed at one of the soldiers who had just shot Hockensmith and pulled the trigger, but the hammer fell on a spent cylinder.

I dropped the Army back into the mud and buried my head in my arms for a moment. It was finally over. I was defenseless and beaten. My other revolvers were still in the hayloft, with my jacket. Then I realized I was lying in my own blood. I tried to sit up, but my body defied me. Then I attempted to get to my feet, and discovered that I couldn't move my hips or my legs—nothing, in fact, below the middle of my chest worked.

That is when I realized that not only had I been shot in

the back, but that the ball had broken my spine. But I didn't have much time to dwell upon this, as the Yankee guerrillas who had killed Glasscock and Hockensmith came riding back. They dismounted and stood over me, laughing. One of them put the toe of his boot beneath my shoulder and turned me over, onto my back.

"Why, he looks kind of like a turtle, don't he?" the man asked, revealing a row of tobacco-stained teeth behind a full beard. "Just lying there in the mud and the blood and flat on his back, unable to get away."

"I can't walk, damn you."

"Well, if that's the case," the bearded trooper said, "then you won't be needing these." He crouched at my feet and grabbed the heels of my boots. The boots were tan-colored and made of fine calf leather, and since they had been stolen at Danville, they were still fairly new.

The other trooper reached down and picked up my Army.

"You really ought to take better care of your pistols," he said. "But this one ought to clean up right well." Then he stuck the gun in his belt while the other trooper sat down, kicked off his own sorry boots, and pulled mine on.

"Those look right nice," the other trooper said.

"They feel fine, too," the bearded one said. "They're broke in real good."

"What else you got on you?" the other trooper asked, squatting beside me and rifling through my pockets. I knew it was useless to fight back; besides, I was pressing my left hand over the stump of my missing finger in an attempt to stanch the flow of blood. The trooper turned my pockets inside out and cussed because he found no money, just the card portrait of Kate King.

"Who's this?" the clean-shaven trooper asked.

"Pass that back," I said. "Please."

The trooper sneered and sent the card flying with a flip of his wrist.

"Get it yourself," he said.

I suggested he do something to himself that is, as far as I knew, medically impossible.

The trooper pulled the Starr revolver from his flap holster and pressed the barrel against my forehead. It was the gun he had used to kill Glasscock. The muzzle was still warm, the gun smelled of machine oil and burned powder, and on the left side of the cylinder I could see the spent chamber that had launched the ball into Dick's brain.

"You've got quite a mouth on you for a cripple," he said.

"Go ahead and bust his melon," the bearded trooper said. "You'd be doing him a favor."

"Hold!" someone shouted from down the lane.

The troopers stood as Edwin Terrell brought his horse abreast. He wore the same red jacket as the others, and his left arm was in a sling. Terrell had coarse black hair, quick dark eyes, and a thin beard. His slouch hat was pinned up on one side in an attempt, I think, to appear jaunty, but the effect was comical instead.

"Who are you?" Terrell asked.

"Clarke," I said. "Captain, Fourth Missouri Cavalry."

"Commanding?"

I nodded.

"What's wrong with you?"

"Shot in the back," I said. "And the hand."

"Did you know he was an officer?" Terrell asked the men.

"Why, no," the bearded trooper said. "He wasn't wearing a jacket, and his shirt seemed ordinary enough. He never said anything about his commission, so we assumed he was an enlisted man."

"Put him in a blanket and carry him up to the house," Terrell said.

They placed me on a lounge on the porch, and then the troopers began to tear apart Wakefield's house, looking for money or anything else worth stealing. Old Wakefield gave thirty dollars in gold to Terrell and his lieutenant, John Thompson, to make them stop.

"Do you know this man?" Terrell asked Wakefield, referring to me.

"No," Wakefield said.

"You're lying," Terrell said. "That nigra blacksmith down by the gate said these men have been staying here on and off for months. And I seem to recall you drinking whiskey with a couple of them when we rode into the lot."

"A great many men, on both sides, have slept in my barn since the war began," Wakefield said. "They don't always tell me who they are. As for drinking with them just now, you know the necessity of sharing a little of whatever you have to make sure your home stays intact."

"So, you're saying he's Captain Clarke from the Fourth Missouri?"

"I never heard him say," Wakefield said. "But if that's who he says he is, I have no reason to doubt him. Tell me, son, are you in any pain?"

"No," I said. "I don't feel anything below my chest at all. My right hand feels peculiar, however."

"That hand needs to be properly bandaged," Wakefield said.

"After we take him to Louisville for interrogation,"

Terrell said. "Tell me, old man, has the killer Quantrill passed through your gate?"

"The guerrilla?" Wakefield asked. "Why, no. I've heard of him, but never seen him."

"How about you, Clarke?" Terrell asked me. "We know Quantrill is in the area. Do you know where he is?"

"Quantrill's a guerrilla," I said. "I'm regular army. Our paths don't cross."

"If you're regular army," Terrell asked, "then what are you doing in the middle of Kentucky with so few men? Shouldn't you be commanding a company?"

"My company was shot up at Nashville," I said. "What you saw when you rode up is what is left of it. We were on our way east to join Lee's army when we were caught in the rainstorm and took refuge in the barn yonder."

"You can't take him to Louisville," Wakefield protested. "He will die on the way."

"The wound is indeed mortal, I fear," I said. "Captain, would you allow me to spend my last afternoon here, on this porch, with a view of these beautiful hills?"

"I cannot afford to leave men behind to guard you," he said. "I must continue my search for Quantrill."

"How far do you think I am going to run in my condition?"

"Some of your men could spirit you away," he said. "A few escaped by hiding in the pond during the fight and then slipping away in brush, it appears."

"I would not allow that," I said. "I am certain to expire and would prefer not to be dragged about the country first. Allow me to remain here, on this happy spot."

"Please," Wakefield said. "Go on your scout and come back at your leisure. The captain has pledged his word and honor to disallow his removal, and I promise to stand good for that as well."

"All right," Terrell said. "But I imagine he will die before I return. In that event, his corpse is yours to bury."

He turned to go, but my curiosity about his sling got the best of me.

"Captain," I said. "What happened to your arm?"

He gave that perturbed look that people have who want to lie, but know they can't because there are people within earshot that would correct them.

"I fell off my horse," he said.

"That surprises me," I said. "I thought circus performers would have better balance."

Wakefield Farm

Old Jim Wakefield sent for a doctor as soon as Terrell was out of sight.

"Sometimes these things are temporary," he told me brightly. "Perhaps the ball can be removed and the use of your legs restored."

"That has not been my experience," I said. "But I will submit to an examination if it will relieve your conscience."

The afternoon was pleasant and a cool breeze reached my position on the porch and I passed the next few hours chatting with Wakefield and waiting for the physician to arrive. Wakefield bandaged my injured hand, then removed my bloody shirt, washed away the worst of the blood, and gave me one of his clean white pleated shirts. Then he threw a blanket over me, even though I wasn't cold, and brought me springwater, for which I was grateful.

Then a buggy pulled up to the house and a fat old coot climbed out, wearing an old-fashioned beaver hat and clutching a battered valise, and announced he was Dr. McClaskey. He asked if I was the patient. I allowed that I was. The man climbed the steps with some difficulty, then drew up a stool and sat huffing and puffing for a moment.

"Should we fetch you a doctor?" I asked.

"I see the injury has not dulled your wit," he said.

"That's good, right?" Wakefield asked.

"Not necessarily," McClaskey said. "Often to lose one's wits is a kindness. Tell me, there was a fight here this morning?"

He took my right hand in his and examined the bandage.

"What did this?" he asked.

"A rifle ball," I said.

He grunted and allowed there was no more to be done for the hand.

"Pity it was your right hand," he said.

"And the trigger finger, no less," I said. "What are the odds?"

"One in ten."

"Oh, you have received a medical education," I said. "Tell me, is ten the standard allotment of digits or should I have more? Do I have one less rib than a woman?"

"You are drunk with shock," the doctor said.

Then he removed the blanket and grasped my feet and asked if there was any sensation. I said there was not. He took a hat pin from his valise and held it up for me to examine.

"Now," he said, "in a moment I'm going to jab the sole of your foot. Tell me when you feel the pain."

"All right," I said. "I'm ready."

A moment or two passed.

"Go ahead," I said.

"I already have," he said. "Do you have any sensation in your calves or thighs, your stomach or sides?"

"No," I said. "Nothing below my upper chest."

The doctor sighed. He roughly pulled the shirt over my head and then slung my torso forward, and asked Wakefield to hold me in that position while he examined the wound. He sighed several more times, talked to himself, and finally pulled the shirt back down.

I could feel nothing.

"The ball entered your left shoulder blade at a severe angle and then broke your spine here," he said, pressing his finger against my sternum, between my nipples. "I can find no exit wound, so the ball must still be lodged somewhere inside you, but damned if I know exactly where. The place where the ball entered is seeping only a little blood and appears relatively clean, but it will suppurate soon enough."

"Sir, what's your prediction?" Wakefield asked.

"The wound is fatal," he said.

"Then death is certain," I said.

"Absolutely," the doctor said. "Four years of war have given me an advanced education in gunshot wounds, and I have never seen a patient recover from such an injury. While you feel little pain now and are clearheaded, the wound will become infected. It will become ugly and purple with spiderwebbed veins as the poison courses through your body. Then you will develop a high fever in which you will become delirious. Pray for the fever to kill you quickly, because if it doesn't, your body will gradually shut down from disuse—you will make water more and more infrequently and your bowels will twist into knots. Your legs will wither away to nothing and even your arms will eventually resemble sticks. Toward the end, you will be begging for death."

Wakefield looked somber.

"Don't be gentle, Doctor," I said. "Tell me the truth."

"The shock," McClaskey said.

"No," I said. "I just want it to be remembered that I faced the inevitable with my spirit undiminished. That is how I want to be remembered—that I was cheerful in the face of death."

"Of course," Wakefield said.

The fat old doctor waited long enough for Wakefield to give him five dollars in gold, and then tamped the beaver hat down on his head and climbed back into the buggy. He urged us not to tell the Yankees of his visit; then he flipped the reins and wheeled the buggy around in the yard and back down the lane toward the Bloomfield-Taylorsville Road.

"Doctors don't know everything," Wakefield said.

"But they know enough," I said.

As the sun was setting, Frank James emerged from the shadows and stepped up onto the porch and sat down on the stool next to my lounge. He placed a bundle in my lap, wrapped in the wine-colored sash with the testicular tassels that I had taken as a prize at Baxter Springs. Inside were two loaded and capped Navy pistols.

"The Yankee redcoats missed these in the loft," he said.

Then he clutched my good hand and pressed it to his cheek.

"Frank, I no longer need these," I said, indicating the pistols. "I have run a long time, but the Yankees have got me at last."

"Dammit, Bill," he said. "I should have been here."

"Then you would be as dead as Glasscock and Hockensmith," I said. "They gave their lives in vain so that I may greedily have a few more moments of life. While I have always been glad to have you with me in a fight, I am thankful that you were elsewhere this morning. Tell me, how many of the original boys remain?"

"There's Allen Parmer and Payne Jones," Frank said. "Bill Hulse, Jack Harris, and Dave Helton. Donnie Pence."

"Good," I said. "Get them out of the war. Find a place to surrender. Don't wait for Virginia."

"Come with us," Frank said. "We've been scouting the country down by Samuel's Depot, and it is a rough and broken land. The Yankees would never find us there."

"It is no use. I will die."

"We can fetch that little Blue gal of yours and things can be peaceful, at least for a spell. You'd have time to write—why, you could even write your memoirs. *Quantrell, by Himself.* What a barn-burner that would be!"

"I'm afraid I have burned my last," I told him. "You are a true friend and a fighter that is full of dash, but I cannot allow myself to be removed from this place. If you do, Terrell will burn this home and treat Old Wakefield harshly, and may even kill him."

Frank hung his head in resignation.

"But you can do something for me," I suggested.

"Anything," Frank said.

"Should this circus monkey Terrell survive the war, kill him."

"Love to," Frank said. "What about the sable Vulcan?"

"Who?"

"The blacksmith, Almstead Jacobs," Frank said. "He is the one that betrayed us. Should I kill him as well?"

"He did not betray us," I said. "We betrayed ourselves by staying in bluegrass country far too long. Besides, when a negro civilian is surprised by a troop of thirty heavily armed riders and they ask if you've seen Rebel guerrillas, do you suppose the first impulse is to lie?"

I returned the sash and the revolvers to Frank, who

tucked the sash with the big tassels inside his shirt and
slipped the guns into his belt. Then he regarded the palms
of his hands with wonder, as they were bloody. I had
rested my right hand on the sash while it had been in my
lap, and the seeping bandage had made it wet with blood.

Instead of wiping the blood on his trousers or otherwise cleaning his hands, Frank stood up straight and gave
me a very deliberate salute with a crimson right hand.

"Thank you," I said, returning the salute.

"If only you'd had a horse . . ."

"Please, Frank," I said. "You'll ruin the mood if you
quote Richard the Third."

Some of the other boys came to visit me later that
night to say good-bye, and then when I survived one
more day, they came back again, and finally I had to tell
them to clear out before Terrell and his red-jacketed crim-
inals returned.

On Friday, Edwin Terrell did return, and his pinched
weasel-shaped face was as red as his shell jacket. He slid
down from the saddle and tore up onto the porch and
pointed his finger at me with the deliberation someone
would aim a loaded gun.

"You are Quantrill!" he stormed.

"Yes," I said. "But Wakefield did not know."

"Where are the rest of your men?"

"Halfway to Missouri by now," I said.

"Dammit," Terrell said. "Well, at least I have the prize
I sought. You can no longer remain here—I must trans-
port you to Louisville in order to display you to my masters. Do I have your cooperation?"

"As long as Old Wakefield remains unmolested, yes."

Accompanying Terrell's men was an old Conestoga
freight wagon pulled by a pair of mules. The wagon was
huge, shaped like a Chinese junk and having about as

much canvas overhead. My first thought was that the wagon must contain a fortune in loot that Terrell had acquired in his two days of scouting, but he said no—the wagon was for me.

I laughed.

"Really?" I asked. "It is a house on wheels."

"It is a prison on wheels," he said. "It has room enough for you, a squad of guards, and physicians if necessary. It is a journey of forty miles, and it is my aim to deliver you to General Palmer personally, and alive."

"Palmer?" I asked.

"The new commander of the Department of Kentucky," he said. "The man who hired me as a captain in his secret police. He decided it was better to wage war against the guerrillas direct instead of punishing their friends and families. He finds that it makes fewer guerrillas in the long run."

"How progressive," I said. "But what happened to the bastard Burbridge?"

"Banished to Tennessee."

A bed of straw was made for me in the very back of the wagon, and blankets thrown over that, and I was placed inside on a mound of pillows. While one of the red-coated troopers drove the mules, two others sat behind him, facing me, their guns at the ready.

Then we set off back down the lane toward the Bloomfield-Taylorsville Road, and I passed beneath the great iron gate with the Flying W for the last time. We turned north and rolled past the blacksmith's shop, but the forge was cold and Almstead Jacobs was not to be seen.

Terrell's men rode before and aft of the Conestoga, and although I know it was a measure to guard against an ambush from my men, the feeling was more like that of an escort or a parade. We had a pleasant journey of four or five miles, mounted a big hill, and crossed a wooden bridge over the Salt River. Word of my capture had spread quickly, and in Taylorsville and every other spot along the way to Louisville there were folks crowded along the road just to get a glimpse of me, and often girls clustered around the back of the wagon and tearfully pressed cards and flowers into my hands.

We stayed the night at Taylorsville, and while there Terrell summoned a couple of surgeons to examine me. It took them only a few minutes to examine the wound and then to concur with McClaskey's verdict of death. In the morning, the Conestoga was deemed too unwieldy and a farm wagon was summoned, and we completed the rest of the journey in that.

On the third or fourth day after I was shot, we entered Louisville. The streets were thick with people—there were many soldiers and merchants, and these were usually hurrying along, but there were also many coloreds who seemed to have no place to take root except on the curb or alongside buildings. I asked one of my guards about this and he said the coloreds had been flocking to Louisville by the thousands, in defiance of the law, which said that slaves in Kentucky were still, well, slaves. Burbridge had attempted to prosecute those who helped the slaves migrate for theft and the slaves themselves for running away, but Palmer, the new commander, had issued different orders. Not only were the prosecutions dropped, but he demanded that coloreds, even runaway slaves, be afforded the same right to travel as whites.

"Louisville is under siege," the guard said, "by an army of color."

We rolled up to Palmer's headquarters at Ninth and Broadway, just north of the L & R Railway Depot. Terrell disappeared into the building and was gone for just a few minutes before he came back out, trailing General Palmer, a rotund man of about fifty with a shock of whiskers growing from his lower lip.

"So, you are Quantrill," he said, approaching the back of the wagon.

"I am," I said. "Or rather, I was."

"You have raised hell from here to Kansas," Palmer said. "A great many people would like to see you dead."

"They have only to wait a little while," I said.

"For that reason," Palmer said, "I defer a trial. You have already been dealt your punishment by man and will soon give a full account to a higher power. Are you in much pain?"

"Surprisingly little," I said.

"I'm glad," Palmer said. "There has been enough suffering all-around."

Then he turned around and saw Terrell lurking behind him, and said: "You have accomplished your mission. You are relieved of duty. Collect your pay and return to whatever it was you did in civilian life, although I fear to know your true vocation."

"There are still guerrillas in the hills," Terrell protested. "At least a dozen more of Quantrill's band are ranging Nelson and Spencer counties. Don't you want them brought in as well?"

"The regular army will deal with them," Palmer said. "You have brought Quantrill to me, your task is done."

Terrell motioned impatiently to his lieutenant, and together they marched back into the headquarters. Then Palmer nodded, and a couple of regular Yankee soldiers lifted me out of the wagon. With an arm around each of their necks, I stood, in a fashion.

"You are bound now for the prison hospital, yonder,"

Palmer said, indicated a building at the corner of Tenth and Broadway. "Corporal, where is that litter? I thought there was a litter coming."

"If you please," I told Palmer, "I'd rather enter upright between these men than be carried in like a butchered hog."

"Of course," Palmer said. "Do I have your word that you will behave yourself?"

"Sir, you do."

"Then I will not order a guard posted," he said. "You may have visitors, as long as they agree not to spirit you away. You will be treated well, or at least as well as can be expected—which is to say, perhaps not very well at all, because there are hundreds of wounded men in that hospital and precious little staff. But I recognize your commission as an officer, and you will be treated as such."

"Thank you for that kindness," I said.

"It is all that can be afforded," Palmer said. "I suggest you make use of what time you have wisely. If you have family, you may wish to send them a few words to remember you by. Make whatever peace with your maker that might comfort you. With that, Captain Quantrill, I bid you farewell—perhaps we will meet again someday on Christ's golden shore."

"Don't count on it," I said.

Book Three

You'll sit on his white neck-bone
And I'll peck out his bonny blue eyes
With a lock of his golden hair
We'll thatch our nest when it grows bare

—"The Twa Corbies," *Scottish folk song*

A Low Diet

My new home was a ward, or pavilion, which was ridge-ventilated and fourteen feet high at the crotch of the eaves and half that at the walls. There was a room at one end for supplies and at the other end for nurses, and crowded between were at least a hundred inmates. A row of barred windows faced Tenth Street, and these were habitually open, as the stench from the inmates and the slop buckets they filled was overpowering. There was one physician and one steward for all hundred inmates; the physician was an officer, and the steward—who mixed the medicine and had been an apothecary before the war—held the rank of warrant officer.

The doctor was a young fool with captain's bars on his shoulders who would come by every morning, ask some ignorant question such as "How are you feeling?" and order a dose of calomel for everyone, whether their bowels were moving or not. Purgative action, no matter how severe, was considered a benefit. Calomel, or mercurous chloride, caused poisoning when given often enough, and unfortunately it was one of the most common drugs because it was cheap; other, more expensive drugs, were not scarce but were given sparingly in the prison hospital.

While men moaned in agony, morphine was rationed quite stingily on the basis that Yankee wounded were more deserving. Most of what we got in the prison hospital was anything that tasted bitter and made us sicker, including assafoetida, pokeweed, and hog's foot oil.

The doctor considered time spent with me as a waste of time, and our conversations were typically even more brief than was customary with the other men. Clearly, he disliked me.

"Still alive, eh?" he would ask.

"Sorry," I would answer. "I'll try not to disappoint tomorrow."

Never did he examine or probe my wounds in any detail, but instead ordered a constant supply of purgatives that he said were to keep my bowels from becoming twisted. Personally, I think it was just an added measure of torture. He also prescribed for me the "low diet," which consisted of rice, farina, toast, and tea. Food was a problem in Louisville during the spring of 1865 and the situation in the prison hospital was no better, so most inmates got a half or low diet anyway, even if they had been recommended the full diet.

I had not much of an appetite, but I did find myself craving coffee.

On my shirt was pinned a tag bearing my name and rank, followed by the designation *guerrilla*. The tags, of course, were provided so that the identity of the inmates could be established upon their death.

The tags were especially useful after the surgeon-in-charge would come on his weekly visit, poke and prod wounds with his thick fingers, and order surgery. Few of the men who were taken away for surgery were seen on the ward again.

Every day or two one of the rough male nurses would

come by and repack the bandage on my back. The dressing was lint, applied wet, and covered with muslin and held in place with plaster. If the nurse could read—which was shockingly rare—he might look at my name tag and give a dismissive chuckle.

"The real Charley Quantrell," he would say, or something similar, "is still whipping Yankees with Sue Mundy down by Samuel's Depot."

There was also a wardmaster, an enlisted man who took his responsibilities as a keeper of prisoners rather more seriously than his function as a member of a hospital staff. The wardmaster, a sergeant named Gruber, organized the nurses, who were drawn from the ranks of the healthy prisoners, and occasionally allowed volunteers from the Louisville Sanitary Commission to assist the nurses in caring for the inmates. These volunteers were, without exception, married (and often matronly) women who were expected to have an ironclad defense against any advance a lonely male patient might attempt.

I hadn't been on the ward more than a few hours before I started hearing stories of Mary Culhain, and from the gossip it was clear the inmates had a low opinion of her. She was a Catholic, which was the first strike against her, she was a woman with an opinion, which was her second strike, and she was reportedly unruffled by any glimpse of male anatomy in the course of her duties, which cinched the deal.

Pride and ignorance are favored vices of even the most desperate of men.

The days passed and I attempted to keep my spirits up, but it became more and more difficult with the grim conditions on the ward and the unrelenting monotony of daily life and my inability to even move from my bed to visit one end of the ward or the other. There were cards, and some of the ambulatory inmates would sometimes come over and play with me, but without money to bet, poker bored me. Also, there were no current newspapers on the ward, except for a few months-old sheets that were used as privy paper.

But the worst thing of all was the indignity of being unable to take care of my personal business, and having to rely on the mercy of the male nurses to clean me as one would a babe in arms. Often, I would not know I needed attention until others would call attention to the smell, which made me feel ever more small.

I had expected to shuffle the mortal coil within a few days, from what the doctors had said about my imminent death. But my mind remained clear and my body, maddeningly stubborn.

After two weeks of this, my spirits were at their nadir and I was thinking that if one of my old comrades could somehow visit me, it might lift my spirit enough to sustain me a few more days—or at least I could beg them to leave me with a contraband revolver or at least a razor with which to take my own life. The thought frightened me, because it betrayed a shocking lack of character.

I tried to banish the thought, but it proved as stubborn as I was.

Then, on the second Friday after I was imprisoned, Mary Culhain appeared.

Mary Culhain

Lady on the floor!" the call came from the far end of
the pavilion. The inmates, who had grown used to the
company of other men and were far from modest in their
behavior, scrambled to pull on shirts and trousers or to
throw blankets over themselves. More than a few pair of
dice and decks of cards were scattered in the commotion,
along with letters and pipes and tobacco and the rest of
the trash that a soldier accumulates in his personal kit.

Mary Culhain held a gloved hand to her nose and
choked a bit as she passed between the beds, but her
stride never slowed. She was no more than thirty, and ath-
letic like a boy, with blue eyes set in a porcelain face that
contrasted with her long dark hair. Around her shoulders
was a dark cape that flared behind her. At her heels was
our wardmaster, the particularly unpleasant Gruber, who
grumbled in German and emphatically pleaded with her
in English to notify him before visiting the pavilion.

"Sergeant Gruber," the woman said, "if I did that, then
you would have time to clean the bedding and scrub the
floor and put fresh dressings on all of the wounds and encourage the inmates to be on their best behavior and to
shoot the ones that refuse full of morphine."

"Well, *ja*," Gruber said.

"That would defeat the purpose of my visits," she said. "The idea is to inspect the ward under the actual conditions the men are subjected to, not have a dress parade for my benefit."

I was surprised that she had no hint of an Irish accent, considering her name, but spoke instead in the flat and broad tones that are peculiar to central Kentucky.

She stopped in the middle of the ward, placed her hands on her hips, and surveyed the rows of crowded beds going in each direction like railway ties.

"The stench here is unbearable," she said.

"It is summer," Gruber said.

"Spring is not yet over," she said. "If sanitation is not improved immediately, then you might as well turn this ward into the death house."

"There is no men," Gruber said.

"Then bring me a bucket," she said. "We will scrub together."

"I do not scrub," Gruber said.

"You will or I will inform the commander," she said.

Gruber walked off, grumbling, to fetch the cleaning supplies.

I watched as this woman removed her gloves and cape and got down on her hands and knees and scrubbed the floor, balls of sweat dripping from the end of her nose. She would occasionally chastise Gruber for not working hard enough, and when a pair of the male nurses came on duty after lunch, he ordered them—with obvious relief—to take over. By the time the floor was done, Mary Culhain's hands and forearms were nearly raw from the work.

But she wasn't done.

Next, she organized the male nurses into a laundry detail, and began stripping the bedding. They worked one side of the ward and she, the other, and she managed a cheerful word for every inmate she encountered, though many met her greeting with indifference.

Her side of the ward happened also to be mine, and my anxiety grew as I watched her help the inmates out of bed and onto the wooden chairs beside the beds as she stripped the sheets and blankets.

When she came to my bed, she wiped the sweat from her face with a handkerchief and smiled. I asked if she was Mary Culhain, and when she allowed that she was, I told her how fond I was of the name, for I had a sister named Mary back home.

"Then I shall attempt to care for you as tenderly as would your sister," she said.

She waited a moment, perhaps expecting me to yield the bed, and when I did not, she begged my pardon.

"Sir, I must gather your bedding," she said. "Could you sit up?"

"I'm afraid not," I said. "My spine is broken."

"Oh," she said. "I am sorry. I should have known."

"I should have said something first," I said, "but I was ashamed to admit my incapacity."

"Place your arms around my neck," she said, "I can help you—"

"I would rather you didn't," I said. "It has been some time since the nurses have attended me. Because I have no sensation, I may have soiled myself without realizing it."

Her eyes softened.

"How long has it been since you've been attended?" she asked.

"Two days," I said.

"Good Lord," she said.

"What is your name?"

I told her.

"The guerrilla?" she asked.

"That's what it says," I said, tapping the tag pinned to my shirt. "You look surprised. Why?"

"The news of your capture by Terrell the Terrible was announced by the *Daily Courier*," she said, "but the report was immediately refuted by the *Democrat*, which said it was a case of mistaken identity and that the genuine Quantrill still rode with Price in Missouri."

"Did they misspell my name?" I asked.

"Pardon?"

"Did they spell my name with an *e* or an *i*?"

"An *e*, I believe."

"Dammit," I said. "Do you think they would misspell the name of Fra Diavola, William de la Marck, or El Empecinado?" Since Lawrence, I had given up comparing myself to Caesar and Washington.

"Do you have a fever?" she asked, touching my brow.

"No," I said impatiently.

"You are making no sense."

"Just go on with the other beds and allow the nurses to care for me when they have the time," I said. "I am in no hurry, as I have no imminent appointments scheduled."

She folded her arms. "You are no longer in charge, Mr. Quantrill."

"Captain Quantrill."

"All right, then, *Captain*," she said. "Not only are you a prisoner and a hospital inmate, but you are badly in need of someone to care for you. I am a married woman and a good Catholic and you have nothing to fear from me."

I snorted.

"Why do you laugh?"

"Madam," I said, "I expect a certain and a mercifully quick death. A woman with a bucket of soap and water holds no terror for me."

"I will not force myself upon you, sir," she said. "And I do not think you are anxious for death, considering your spirits. But I can tell you this: For a wounded man, soap and water is his primary defense against a quickly worsening condition. And even if, as you say, death is imminent, I would want to spend my last days or hours in a fresh bed with clean clothes. But the decision is yours, to either lie in your own filth or accept some small help from a woman."

She stood staring at me for a moment, her hands on her hips, sweat coating her brow. Then, impatient because I had not yet answered, she swept the covers back.

"That you considered it was answer enough," she said.

Not so Much

Mary Culhain knew things that even the doctors were ignorant of.

She explained that to keep my bladder and bowels working, she would have to knead my abdomen and stimulate my nether regions. I was mortified by this suggestion, and assured her that a gentleman would never allow such inappropriate touching. She just smiled and said to let her know when I changed my mind.

In three days, having no bodily sensation but feeling poorly and knowing that something was seriously wrong in my guts, I relented. So began a daily ritual that never became easy for me—or, I daresay, for her—but which became less uncomfortable with time. During the regimen, I would focus my mind on something else—conjugating Latin verbs, for example, or attempting to remember all of the words to a favorite song.

But there was no privacy on the ward and the routine remained shocking to others; the doctors often said that such effort was not only wasted, but unseemly, and the male nurses said that if the duty ever fell to them, I would surely die.

Then one day when the men in the beds around mine

were quite asleep, she went further, and asked if I had any awareness of my male member; I assured her that I did not and asked her why she would ask such a question.

"Captain," she said, "surely you have noticed that it answers roll call nearly every morning. I was just curious about the mechanism that is responsible for this, since the reaction is divorced from desire."

"May I ask how you are so sure?"

"Because it is sometimes necessary to take your member in hand during the normal course of maintaining your sanitation," she said, "and never does a reaction cross your face."

I turned my face away.

"I'm sorry," she said. "I was curious."

"I think of the women I knew, sometimes," I said.

"Do you miss it?"

"Not the act so much," I said.

"Were there many?"

"A few," I said. "Some whores out West, red and white and in between. A woman named Annie Walker in Missouri early in the war, and later, another named Kate King, a child really, but with whom I passed a few pleasant months. A girl here in Kentucky."

"But you married none of them?"

"No," I said.

"Do you miss them?"

"I miss the closeness, the nearness of them, the way their skin was smooth and fresh," I said. "How they looked in the moonlight. But this makes me sad, so let's talk of something else."

"All right," she said. "What?"

"Why do you do this?" I asked.

"Captain," she said, "if I didn't do this, then who would?"

"Obviously, none," I said. "But this is not something that a woman simply wakes up one day with an urge to do. 'Oh, I think I'll go down to the prison infirmary and care for the most hopeless cases.' "

"No," she said.

"Then why?"

"Because it is what Christ would do," she said.

"Well, it would be a little easier for Him," I said. "Just walk into the pavilion and heal everybody. No need to get one's hands dirty."

"Do not blaspheme," she said.

"I have found little comfort in religion."

"Then perhaps you should look again," she said.

"What a strange woman you are," I said. "You untwist my bowels with your hands, you quiz me about the windage of my loose cannon, and you chastise my approach to religion. I confide to you my most tender details, and yet you become like ice when I inquire about your life."

She sighed.

"I'm unhappy," she said. "My marriage . . . but many women are."

"Some aren't."

"No," she said. "They are widows."

Shocked, she placed a hand over her mouth.

"What else?"

"The war has also made me unhappy," she said. "The waste of men and boys, the misery of the wives and girlfriends, the food shortages and the uncertainty and how miserable Louisville has become. I am unhappy with slavery, and that as a nation we have lagged so far behind Britain and France in abolishing it. Yes, I know. Don't give me that look."

I shrugged.

"I am not who people think I am," I said.

"Who are you, then?"

"It would take a very long time to explain," I said. "And I'm certain I don't have that much time."

"Then start near the end," she suggested. "Tomorrow I will bring a paper and pencil, and you can write until you are no longer able, and then you can dictate to me. I have a good memory, am a champion speller, and have some interest in the subject."

"I would be prone to lie," I said.

"Not to me, you wouldn't."

I hesitated.

"You'll want to know about Lawrence, of course," I said finally. "Everybody does."

Dry Leaves

So that is how it began, with the captain writing his own story at first, and only later dictating to me when the writing proved too difficult. His spirits were high in the beginning, his mind was sharp, and his color and demeanor were that of a healthy individual; if one did not know of the paralysis, one would assume he had just taken to bed for a little nap. He kept his blond hair combed and his mustache trimmed, and his manners were those of a gentleman.

I would come before breakfast or after supper, so that I could continue my work caring for the other men, and we would talk about what he had written, and sometimes I would ask him a question here or there.

From the start, I wanted to know what he had seen at Lawrence that he could not talk about; I had seen so much suffering since becoming a matron that I believed nothing could shock me. We also talked about the language of men, which he had honestly recorded, and he was apologetic. But I told him it was one of those things that everybody knows but few discuss, that to soften the language would be doing a disservice to the truth, and that such language was appropriate because he was producing a *private* memoir.

But the captain became weaker as the days passed, as I knew he must, and though I tried to keep the wound in his back clean and dressed, it was an open wound, and eventually began to fester. Although he never gave in to pessimism, his mood gradually lowered, and a wry sort of fatalism appeared. He also became easily fatigued, so I took over the duties of writing as he described events, and I did my best not only to accurately record his recollections, but to mimic his writing style. Then, as he became listless and he lost interest or was unable to groom himself, I took over those duties as well.

By the end of May, a full three weeks had passed since he had taken the Spencer ball in the back, and although he had become fatigued and unable to fully care for himself, there was yet plenty of hope; the captain exhibited no signs of fever or inflammation of the lung, which of course we now call pneumonia, and he had even escaped the scourge of every soldier, the flux, also known as diarrhea.

The fever came with the month of June, as the weather became warmer and it became more and more difficult to keep his wound clean. The captain's mind—which had been remarkably clear—became clouded and sometimes jumbled the pages of time. He would talk about events he had already described, or give new information or an account that conflicted with what had gone before, and I tried my best to make a coherent and chronological narrative from the notes I took at his bedside.

He also described things that I was sure had not happened—the meeting with the washerwoman when seeking a way out of the slough in the Land Between, for example, and the tale of Hyacinth Fugate, the girl with the blue skin with whom he claimed to have spent the night before being shot at Wakefield Farm. While I did not think the captain was lying, I knew that he was a widely read man, and thought that his mind had woven bits and pieces of fairy tales into the story of his life.

The fever increased rapidly each day until, on the third or fourth day of June, with the fever baking his skull, he announced he was finished with the memoir. I was sitting at his bedside, a pencil and paper in hand, and uttered some small protest.

"But we don't know how it ends," I said.

"It ends where men's lives usually end—with death," he said. "I leave it to you to provide a postscript to the narrative describing the particulars."

Then I pressed him for details that I felt were needed to complete the narrative, and chiefly what he had seen in Lawrence that was so grim that it had so haunted his dreams.

"Words are dry leaves in my mouth," he said. "No more."

When the doctor came by that morning, I asked if nothing could be done. Impatiently, he turned the captain on his side, removed the dressings, and inspected the wound. It was swollen with pus and the edges were the color of eggplant. It also stank of putrefaction. The doctor shook his head.

"If only we could remove the ball," he said.

Then he thrust his index finger into the wound, all the way to the knuckle, and probed around a bit. The captain must have felt something, for his body shuddered and he uttered a most pitiful moan.

"I do not feel it," he said, removing his hand and wiping the blood and pus on a rag that he took from his pocket. "The only hope is surgery—and the chances, Mrs. Culhain, are slim."

"But there is some chance?" I asked.

I knew better, but was desperate for any small hope—even a lie.

"Perhaps," he said. "We will give him over to the surgeons."

"Captain," I said when the doctor had gone. "Do you understand?"

"I am to die," he said.

"That is not for certain."

"It is, for all of us," he said. "Sooner for some than others."

"Well, we must try."

"And try we will," he said. "Mrs. Culhain, there is a woman in Missouri I want you to contact—Olivia Cooper. She holds eight hundred dollars for me, and I wish my mother and sister to receive the money."

"Of course," I said. "Where do I find her?"

"Missouri," he said.

"But where in Missouri?"

He did not answer.

Early on the morning of the fifth of June, he was placed on a litter and carried down to the operating table, where he was given a shot of whiskey and then a sponge saturated with chloroform was held beneath his nose. I hope he enjoyed the whiskey, for I am sure he would not remember the chloroform. When the patient was limp from the anesthetic, the surgeons began their work.

I did not witness the operation, but I had seen others like it. The surgeons would have prepared for the operation by scrubbing everything down with Labarraque's solution—everything, that is, except their hands and instruments, because the solution was strong bleach and made their hands itch. Now, even a schoolboy recognizes the folly of such an approach, but this was some years before germ theory was accepted as fact. If only the surgeons had used the sodium hypochlorite that we matrons did to scrub the floor and urinals, many a patient would have been saved.

But, at the time, the emphasis was on *cutting*.

I had kept track of the odds of mortality following surgery in my time at the hospitals, and the numbers were of no comfort; about one in three patients died, and the odds worsened the closer to the trunk an operation was. A soldier who had a leg removed at the hip would die eight times out of ten; for any kind of surgery of the torso, including the back, the odds of recovery or death were about even, but there was a wild card—the more time that had passed since the wound was received, the less of a chance the patient had of recovering. Again, the more time that had passed since a wound, the better the chance of it becoming infected.

But there were a lucky few patients who had posted recoveries against the longest of odds.

Sadly, the captain was not to be counted among them.

When they carried him back to his bed on the ward, the captain was unconscious. The surgeon was with him, still wearing the stained apron he wore while operating. Blood was caked beneath his fingernails and splattered across the tops of his shoes.

"We could not find the ball," he said. "We had believed it might be resting just beyond the spine, but it has lodged itself far more deeply. Madam, I am sorry, but we did our best."

The surgeon left and I sat alone with the captain for a

time, watching his ragged breathing. Then near ten
o'clock he woke with a start and his hands reached for
pistols that were no longer at his waist, and he looked
wildly about until he saw my face.

"The Lawrence nightmare?" I asked.

He nodded.

I fetched some water from the barrel and held the cup
to his cracked lips, and he took a few swallows. Then he
looked at me and asked, in a hoarse voice, how much
time he had left.

"Not long," I said. "A day, perhaps."

Then, to my surprise, he asked me to fetch a priest.

I sent Gerber to retrieve Father Michael Power, one of
the prison hospital's chaplains. Then I told the captain the
priest was coming, and he nodded.

"Thank you for every kindness," he said. "You have
cared for me as a mother should care for her son."

"Don't speak," I said.

"But I must," he said, then coughed. It was a wet
cough, as his lungs were filling with fluid. "The money
from the Cooper woman—buy a plot and headstone for
me. Send the rest to Kate King. And your question about
Lawrence," he said, "the thing I saw—the answer is
there."

"Where?" I asked.

"A few pages, hidden beneath the seat," he said. "I
wrote them weeks ago, but was too cowardly to share
them with you."

I felt beneath the chair, and found the pages, which
had been folded in half and tacked to the bottom. When I
began to unfold the pages, he shook his head.

"When I pass," he said. "Not before."

Then Gruber came in leading Father Power, who
kissed his stole and slipped the silken yoke around his

neck. In his hand was a small valise that contained the holy water and other things he would need.

By necessity, the sacrament was abbreviated to its most essential form—the priest asked if the captain desired baptism in the name of the Father, the Son, and the Holy Ghost. With some difficulty, the captain affirmed that he did. Then Father Power produced a vial of holy water, sprinkled a few drops on the captain, and placed a hand on his forehead and renounced Satan—completing the first sacrament.

Then Father Power proceeded to give the captain last rites.

"No confession?" the captain croaked.

"Could you undertake a full confession?"

"That would take a few weeks," he said.

"Then, I must simply ask you this: Are you in a state of genuine contrition?"

"Yes," the captain said, then coughed. "My remorse is severe."

"Then you are absolved," the priest said, then wet his thumb from a vial of oil and pressed the thumb to the captain's forehead. "Through this holy unction may the Lord pardon thee of whatever sins or faults thou has committed," he said in Latin.

Then he asked if the captain could take food, and when I told him no, he produced from the valise a tiny bottle of consecrated wine, uncorked it, and poured a bit into a tin cup.

"Lift his head," the priest said.

As I cradled the captain, the priest opened the captain's mouth and poured a bit of the wine into it. "This is the viaticum," he said gently. "This is to sustain you during your three-day journey to the next world, and to assure you that you die with Christ, who promises eternal life."

The captain took a couple of labored breaths.

He attempted to speak, and Father Power had to lean down to understand the words. The captain spoke briefly; then his head fell back in exhaustion.

"What did he say?" I asked.

"Now I'm oiled—keep me from the rats."

Because the captain's soul was now in the care of the Catholic Church, his body was delivered to them as well, so that the United States government would not bear the expense of burial. He was removed that day to St. Joseph's Infirmary on Fourth Street, which was operated by the Sisters of Charity of Nazareth.

The infirmary had been built in the 1830s and, unlike the new military hospitals with their pavilion design, St. Joseph's packed the patients—mostly poor Germans and Irish—into rooms that seemed quite small in comparison. The captain was given a bed in one corner, and from the time he arrived, I kept the death vigil.

He survived the night and lingered for much of the next day. But then, just after four o'clock in the afternoon, his eyes fluttered open and he reached for my hand.

"Boys, get ready," he said in a clear voice. "Steady!"

Then his eyes clouded, his breathing stopped, and he died.

He was twenty-seven years old.

I closed his eyes and smoothed his hair, then sat for perhaps an hour beside him before summoning one of the sisters and asking her to summon an undertaker. Then, as the day grew long, I waited with him for the undertaker to arrive.

It must have been six o'clock or later when I became

aware of someone standing nearby, staring silently at the captain's corpse. It was a girl, about sixteen, in a cheap but clean gingham dress. She had straight red hair and dark eyes, her hands were clasped over her stomach, and her skin was decidedly blue.

"Hyacinth Fugate?" I asked.

"Yes, ma'am," the girl said. "But call me Blue. Are you . . . are you his wife?"

"No," I said. "The captain is . . . the captain was unmarried."

"Are you a friend?" she asked.

"Of sorts," I said. "A volunteer matron."

"Ah," Blue said, and took a few steps forward. "What's that?"

"Someone who helps the wounded soldiers."

She nodded.

"I heard about his capture, and how he was wounded and taken here to Louisville," she said. "It took me a couple of weeks to decide to come here, and another week to walk here, and this must be the biggest goddamned place in all of God's creation. So many pink people. Then, when I finally found the prison hospital, they told me he'd been moved here. I haven't seen him since . . ."

"That day?" I asked.

She nodded.

"The captain told me."

She smiled.

"There was something I wanted to tell him that morning," she said, and then bit her lip. "But we had a bargain not to say farewells or discuss the future, so I didn't. But it doesn't make any difference now, does it? He's dead and can't hear me."

"What did you want to say, Blue?"

"That I carry his child," she said. "I really wasn't sure at first, so maybe that's why it kind of stuck in my throat, but now I'm damned sure."

"Oh Lord," I said.

"He didn't have nothin' to do with it."

"What can I do for you, child?" I asked. "The child should be recognized as his, because I understand there is a sum of money in question, and you need a place to live and raise the child. . . ."

"No, ma'am," she said. "I don't need none of that. I shift for myself. Me and my pink baby will be just fine. I just wanted to tell Captain Quantrill so that he would know—not that he would pay me off or promise to do the right thing or any of a dozen dumb-ass things men say in such situations. There's not a thing I want, not even his name. I just wanted to say good-bye, and to thank him."

"I'm sure he would have appreciated it."

"He'll be buried decent?"

"Yes," I said. "That is one of the things I promised."

She smiled. "Want to touch my skin?"

"Yes," I said. "I do."

She walked over and offered her right hand, and I took it gently in my own. I caressed her forearm and examined the skin and concluded that her color was indeed natural.

"Peculiar, ain't it?" she asked. "But it ends with me."

Then she said farewell, turned, and threaded her way through the beds toward the doorway. As she was going out, Father Power was coming in, to tell me that the undertaker was finally on his way, but when he saw Blue Fugate, he stopped and stared as she passed.

Then he came over to where I sat next to the body.

"Who was that imp?" he asked.

"A girl the captain loved," I said. "She is with child."

Father Power crossed himself.

"Good Lord," he said. "It will be the Antichrist."

Lawrence Reprise

It is a boy, perhaps fifteen, faceup in the street with arms and legs bent at joint-busting angles. He is still alive, and drunken Dick Glasscock with his bald head and cannibal smile is standing behind him with his great knife. Glasscock tears the shirt from the boy's back. Then he plunges the knife into the boy and twists the blade, and I can hear the breaking of ribs.

Glasscock throws me a wicked smile.

"Bill, is this how they did it in the old days?"

He uses both hands to hack and lever ribs away from the spine, then removes the knife and plunges his right hand into the gash. He pulls out a flap of grayish pink material that hangs weirdly, and the ribs are fanned out like some kind of macabre wing. Then Glasscock repeats the process on the other side, and the two inner wings move at the same time the boy fights for breath. I realize the things are his lungs.

"Look what I made," Glasscock says. "An angel from an abolitionist!"

The boy gasps and shudders and for a moment his wide eyes meet mine, pleading. I am stunned, and cannot react. Finally, when my hand reaches for the butt of the

Army, a rifle booms behind me and the boy takes the ball squarely in the forehead and his brains dribble out the back of his skull.

The wings are now thankfully still.

I glance behind me and there is Honey John standing in the street, the Sharps in his hand, a cloud of white smoke drifting to one side.

"Why didn't you stop that, Bill?" Honey John asks.

I would like to say I pulled the Army and shot Glasscock in the chest, that he dropped the knife and staggered backward in surprise. That I sent two more shots into his chest, and that he crumpled next to the boy.

But I don't touch the Army. I turn away.

Honey John shakes his head and walks away.

I move on toward Jim Lane's house, and when I come back this way the body has been trampled. The boy is now missing his trousers and one of his shoes. The pink toes of his left foot are smeared with mud. His abdomen has been crushed, and his manhood displaced. His neck has a gash so large that it exposes the gleaming white jawbone.

Two large and very black crows are perched atop the boy's chest, teasing stringy bits of flesh from the neck wound. A mangy yellow dog is sniffing and slobbering over the insult to a groin.

I nudge Charley forward, and the crows protest and flap their wings, and hop away from the boy. Finally, they take flight. The dog, however, is reluctant to yield. The dog snarls as I urge Old Charley closer. Charley dislikes dogs and he approaches in a sideways prance, bobbing his head vigorously to express his displeasure.

The dog snarls, but I nudge Old Charley forward and leave the beast to its meal.

Sub Rosa

The captain was buried on June 7 in an unmarked grave in the south half of lot 624 at the edge of St. Mary's Catholic Cemetery at Portland, behind the home of the cemetery caretaker, Patrick Shelly. The witnesses were Shelly, his wife, Bridget, and a grave digger named Wertz.

Being the only one present that had actually known the captain, I must be counted as the only authentic mourner. Fitting my role, I was dressed in black and held a single red rose in my hands.

Father Power had determined that funeral rites at graveside would suffice, because the captain had been a Catholic for only a short time—and was notorious for Lawrence and Baxter Springs. Because Father Power was busy with his infirmary duties and could not attend even the cemetery rites, his colleague, Father Brady, was kind enough to officiate. But, as a consequence of Father Brady never having met the deceased, his words were brief.

After some boilerplate about the redemptive power of Christ, the priest read a fragment of the Requiem. The relevant portion, roughly translated from my imperfect

Latin, was: "Day of wrath, a day that the world shall dissolve in ashes, as foretold by David and the Sibyl . . ."

I have always thought it strange that the Church would draw upon a pagan oracle to lend support to the Christ's judgment, but it goes back to Augustine. Equally strange, I thought, was that the passage which Father Brady had selected as chastisement—the day of wrath and ashes were undoubtedly linked in his mind to Lawrence and punishment—was one of the few passages the captain would find hopeful, because it referenced Augustine.

When Father Brady was finished, he snapped his book shut, flung some Holy Water on the grave, and strode away. The Shellys followed.

The grave was alarmingly shallow—no more than three or four feet.

When I asked grave digger Wertz about this, he said he didn't have time to make it any deeper—there were four poor Irish children he had yet to place into the "public grounds," or pauper's field, which was the normal destination for those from the city poorhouse and asylum, a block to the west. Also, Wertz said, it was the custom to make unmarked graves shallow.

Then I asked why the grave was to be unmarked, and Wertz said he was following directions. Father Power was afraid that the body might be exhumed by the curious or the hateful, he said, and that it was best to make it as inconspicuous as possible. The silver, if there indeed was any, would be used later to erect the monument, as the captain had requested, when the time was appropriate.

After Wertz had finished tamping the grave flat, he shouldered his spade. I gave him fifty cents for his trouble, all I could afford, and he seemed genuinely grateful.

"You will remember this spot, won't you?" I asked. "Lest everyone else forget, you will mark it?"

"For you, madam," he said, tugging the brim of his hat. "Just for you."

After he walked away I stood for some moments regarding the fresh gave. Then I knelt, said the Lord's prayer, and placed the single red rose atop the mound of earth.

I visited the grave again on July 31, the captain's birthday, to deliver another rose. To my horror, I discovered that the Shellys had taken to throwing their dishwater and night soil out of their kitchen window onto the grave. They said it was an attempt to obscure the grave, and to keep if from being desecrated, but I was not so sure. It seemed more a comment on the captain's life than any attempt to preserve his memory.

In time, however, the Shellys tired of this game, and the captain's grave simply became part of the grassy yard between the caretaker's house and the iron gate that separated the cemetery from Duncan Street.

Hateful Things

In the twenty years and more since placing that first rose upon Captain Quantrill's unmarked grave, I have kept track of those who played parts both large and small in his short and brutal earthly drama.

In the margins of the yellowed manuscript that the captain dictated to me, I have made careful notes in the cases where the fates of some of those individuals are known, either by being published in the newspapers or by reliable accounts relayed by witnesses with whom this recorder is acquainted.

I didn't have long to wait to make the final entry for Edwin Terrell, the red-clad guerrilla hunter who surprised the captain at Wakefield Farm. In the months immediately following the war he continued to rob and murder, and in September of 1866 he was arrested for the murder of an Illinois stock trader whose body had been pulled to the surface of Clear Creek by a fisherman. He escaped that charge because of a hung jury, but he was immediately jailed at Taylorsville to await trial for the murder of a blacksmith. On April 13, some members of the old red-coated gang kidnapped the jailer and forced him to free Terrell, who fled to Shelbyville. A posse cornered Terrell,

who resisted arrest, and while fleeing was promptly rid-
dled with rifle and shotgun fire. One ball struck him in
the back at the spinal column and emerged near his
collarbone, and was judged to be fatal.

Terrell was taken to Louisville, partially paralyzed and
in crippling pain.

But months later—after somehow surviving and having been released from the charges of killing the blacksmith—Terrell was admitted to the Louisville City
Hospital, where he hoped surgeons could provide some
relief by removing the "hateful things" from his back, the
rifle balls and buckshot. He had wasted away so that
those who visited him reported that his arms and his paralyzed legs looked like twigs, that his bowels were
frozen, and that he was racked with such pain that every
quarter of an hour or so he would curl into a ball and
plead for death.

The surgery recovered none of the hateful things from
his body.

On the morning of Thursday, December 13, Terrell
asked for whiskey and then died. He was twenty-three.

He was buried in the pauper's cemetery of the City
Alms House, adjacent to St. Mary's Catholic Cemetery
where the captain slept. A fortnight later, a man claiming
to be Terrell's brother had the body exhumed and said he
was going to ship the body to Missouri for reburial, but
that is curious because Terrell had no family in Missouri.

The final resting place of Edwin Terrell is unknown, at
least to me.

The fates of the boy, the captain, and the other Missouri
boy called "Dingus" have been chronicled elsewhere. As
any newspaper reader knows, Jesse James was the most
famous of the Western outlaws and was assassinated by
Robert Ford on April 2, 1882, at St. Joseph, Missouri.

His brother, Frank James, surrendered and was tried in 1883 for the murder of a passenger during a train robbery, but was acquitted by a Gallatin, Missouri, jury.

Frank James is now selling shoes in Vernon County, Missouri.

Jim Lane, the famed abolitionist who escaped the Lawrence raid by hiding in a cornfield, lived only a year longer than Quantrill. Beset by political, financial, and emotional difficulties, he put a pistol to his head and shot himself on a road near Leavenworth on July 1, 1866.

Eventually, I set the manuscript aside and attempted to concentrate on other things. It had been a generation since, as a young woman, I had sat by the captain's bedside and recorded what pieces of his life he had cared to share with me. The story was done. A generation had passed and Quantrill's boys had been transformed either into dead outlaws or middle-aged men who had grown fat around the middle and liked to talk about the worst days of their lives as if they were the best.

Time had transformed me as well.

I had passed my fiftieth birthday, and avoided mirrors because I did not recognize myself in them; I had not grown fat, as many women do, but I had certainly grown old, and my face had become creviced and cracked like dry saddle leather. The only consolation was that my hateful husband had died of pneumonia in the winter of 1867, leaving me the house in Portland and a small pension and plenty of time to read and think.

And then, and then . . .

One blustery afternoon in December of 1887, there came a knock on my door and I opened it to find a man of about fifty standing on the top step, hat in hand. He was an anxious man with ink-stained hands and when he asked if I was Mary Culhain, I said no. I was in the process of shutting the door in his face when he threw a question inside: "But you knew Quantrill?"

I left the door open a crack.

"Why do you want to know?" I asked.

"Madam," he said. "I am William Walter Scott of Dover, Ohio. I was a boyhood friend of William Clarke Quantrill. I am gathering material for a biography of the infamous guerrilla's life."

"He spoke of you," I said.

"Then you are Mary Culhain?"

"You were his friend, the printer's devil."

"I am now editor of the *Iron Valley Reporter*," he said.

"That must please you."

"I understand from Bridget Shelly, the sexton at St. John's Catholic Cemetery—it was known as St. Mary's during the war—that you spent some time with Quantrill before his death and that he may have shared certain information with you," Scott said. He looked past me at the parlor inside, as if eager for its warmth, but I was reluctant to admit him. "If that is so, I would be keenly interested in hearing what the man may have told you upon his deathbed."

"I don't remember," I said. "It was a long time ago, Mr. Scott."

"Pity," he said. "There are many unanswered questions about his life and his death, and there is such a mania among the public, both North and South, for any scrap of new information, whether one considers him a hero or the devil himself, that I was hoping we could come to terms."

"Terms?" I asked.

"Yes," he said. "I am not a rich man, but I would be able to provide some token in exchange for whatever memories you might be able to recover. The Shelly woman also said she remembered some type of letters or possibly a manuscript that you had in your possession at the time of Quantrill's burial, and if so, the remuneration for that would be considerably more."

"So you want to buy the captain's story?"

"Yes," he said.

I pressed the door once again to shut it. Scott put just enough pressure on the opposite side to prevent me from fully closing it.

"Mrs. Quantrill would like to meet you," he said.

I stopped.

"His wife?" I asked.

"His mother," Scott said. "She has come here to learn the details of her eldest son's death and would be grateful for any information you could provide about his last days."

"Good Lord," I said. "The woman must be ancient."

"She is sixty-eight," he said.

"And why is she coming now, after all of these years?"

"Her days are not many," he said. "She would like to know the truth about her son before she dies."

Scott took a card from his pocket and thrust it toward me. On it was the address of one of the cheaper hotels in downtown Louisville.

"We will be staying for two days, and Mrs. Quantrill would be grateful if you could call at your earliest convenience," Scott said. "And while I would be personally grateful for such a visit, I must warn you: The old woman is considered quarrelsome by many."

The next day the weather turned bitter and I bundled myself tightly and walked downtown to Monroe Street, near the river. All the way I clutched the manuscript, which I had wrapped in brown paper and done up with twine, and the weight of it seemed to slow my progress.

The lobby of the hotel smelled like cigars and old spittoons At the desk, I asked for the number of Mrs. Quantrill's room, and was told there was no guest registered under that name. Then I asked for W. W. Scott, and when the clerk nodded, asked if there was an old woman with him. The clerk directed me to a room at the end of the hall on the third floor.

As I walked up the old and creaky staircase, I pressed the manuscript tightly against my stomach, and I was seized with a sudden apprehension. Despite having walked more than a mile in the freezing cold, I was now sweating. At the landing between the second and third floors I paused to remove my coat. There was a north-facing window on the landing and I stood for a few moments and looked out over the Ohio River. How different it was than during the war, when bonfires lit up the Kentucky bank and gunboats were clustered around Corn Island and a pontoon bridge stretched to the Indiana shore.

Now a locomotive was chugging across the massive iron bridge that cut across the tip of Corn Island above the Falls. The engine belched geysers of white smoke into the sky as it pulled its string of freight cars toward Indianapolis.

At the room, I shifted the manuscript to my left hand and draped my coat over that arm before knocking. After a few moments, a particularly grating voice came through the closed door:

"Who's there?"

"Mrs. Quantrill?" I asked. "It's Mary Culhain. I am here at the invitation of Mr. Scott—"

The door opened abruptly and I was staring into a pair of dark eyes set in a dour face.

"Scott!" she said. "Why, he's not worth the powder it would take to blow him to hell. He's told me nothing but lies for twenty years and I reckoned it was time to come see the truth for myself."

"May I come in?"

She looked me up and down, and then waddled back to her upholstered chair.

"Suit yourself," she said over her shoulder.

I entered the room and politely shut the door behind me, then looked for a place to sit. There was a straight-backed chair beside a table, and on the table was a dried-up sausage and a few slices of an apple that had turned corrupt. I sat at the table, then placed the manuscript on the floor, with my coat over it.

"It is a singular experience to finally meet you," I said. "Do you remember the last time you heard from Bill?"

"You mean Will?" she asked. "The last letter I got from him was written from Kansas Territory before the war. After that, nothing. I believed he died out West. Didn't know he was in the war."

"Pardon me," I said. "Did you not read the newspapers?"

"Waste of time," she said. "Don't understand what anybody sees in it. Now, somebody writes you a letter, that's meant for you. Might have something important to tell you, or might contain money. But a newspaper? It's silly to read things written by strangers."

"Do you mean to say you did not know that the William Quantrill that burned Lawrence was your son?"

"Still don't know," she said. "Have seen no evidence of it, just a bunch of talk from strangers and that regular blather that Scott fellow keeps up about writing a book."

"Mrs. Quantrill," I said gently, "I believe the man I knew at the hospital may indeed have been your son. He confided certain information about family life that only he would know. As an example, he told me he had a sister named Mary that he seemed quite close to. He often wondered how she fared."

"Died in 1863," she said.

"Mary, the invalid sister?" I asked.

"Her spine was curved."

"My God, she had been dead for two years when the captain was wrestling with the thought of sending her a letter," I said. "And his brother Thomas . . ."

"Dead," she spat. "Sent him to Kansas years ago to find out what happened to Will, but he got into some trouble out there and I never did learn the full story."

"So you assume he's dead, but you don't know?"

"That's right," she said; then her demeanor changed like clouds passing across the sun. "You ask a lot of questions but you've been damn short with answers. Tell me again who you are."

"I am Mary Culhain," I repeated. "He struck up a conversation with me because I had the same name as his sister. I nursed him while he lay paralyzed in the hospital here."

She stared at me with those dark birdlike eyes.

"Do you not want to know anything of his passing?"

She thought for a moment.

"Did he leave any money?" she asked.

The question so startled me that I could not speak for several long seconds, and by the time I had recovered my thoughts the door opened and Walter William Scott strode unannounced into the room. His hat was jammed tightly upon his head, his collar was turned up, and beneath his right arm was a ball-shaped object wrapped in newspaper.

"I had to pay the grave digger a dollar, on top of the two dollars I gave that shrewish Shelly woman," he said, his back turned, as he shut the door. "But finally we have satisfaction. It did not take long, for the grave was not deep."

Then he turned and saw me, and his face grew red.

"Pardon me," he told Mrs. Quantrill. "I was unaware that you were entertaining a guest."

"I don't remember her name," the old woman said.

"I know who she is," Scott said, removing his hat and placing the object wrapped in newspapers upon the table next to the dirty plate. "I called upon her yesterday, and I believe that is the reason for her visit today."

"How do you do, Mr. Scott?"

"Very well, thank you," he said, drawing up another straight-backed chair. "Have you been talking long?"

"No," I said. "In fact, I just arrived."

"Good," he said. "Very good indeed."

Then he cocked his head in the way that men do when they are about to impose a change of subject.

"Would you indulge me for a few minutes, Mrs. Culhain? You see, I am rather pressed for time and there is a matter which I must take up immediately with Mrs. Quantrill."

"Then you must excuse me," I said, standing.

"No," he said, placing a hand upon my arm. "I think you may find what I have to show Mrs. Quantrill of some interest."

I nodded and sat. My heart was thumping against my ribs and the flushed feeling had returned and I feared that Scott would reach for the object wrapped in newspaper, which of course he did. But I could not now force myself to protest or to leave, with the thing so near to being exposed.

Scott held the package in both hands.

"Are you faint of heart?" he asked me.

"No," I said, barely able to form the words.

"Understood," Scott said, and removed the newspaper. "Behold the man."

Then I was staring into the empty orbits of a yellowed and grinning skull. The mandible and both rows of teeth were still accounted for and the crown had achieved a patina that reminded me of a tortoiseshell. A few clods of black cemetery dirt clung to the cheekbones and in back hung a patch of hair that had turned a ghostly white.

Then I noticed that one of the lower front teeth was chipped.

I bit my lower lip to keep from crying out.

Then I glanced over at the old woman, who was undergoing the most peculiar transformation. Her features softened and her eyes became damp and for a moment I could believe that there once burned a mother's love in her heart. She reached out with a shaking and wrinkled left hand with fingers like sausages and touched the chipped tooth.

"Will," she said. "It is my Will."

Scott nodded and made a move to wrap the thing in newspaper again.

"No, don't," she said. "Let me gaze upon it for a while. The chipped tooth. The chipped tooth . . . He did that himself when he tripped over his shoes and struck the fireplace iron."

Scott was staring at me.

"Your lip," he said. "It's bleeding."

I touched my fingertips to my bottom lip and they came away bloody.

"It's nothing," I said, and drew a kerchief from my pocket.

"I must return it soon," he said, then gave me a quick smile. "I only borrowed it so that Mrs. Quantrill could be positive that the remains were of her son. You see, we have no authority for an *exhumation* as such."

"As such," I said.

"The coffin is all but gone," he said. "As are the clothes, save for the buttons. Many of the bones have crumbled to dust, but there are some long bones that remain intact."

"He must return to Canal Dover," the old woman said.

"We cannot," Scott said. "It would be a crime."

"We must find a way," she said. "And the rest of the corpse, as well . . ."

They were a pair of crows fighting over a scrap of meat.

"Forgive me," I said. "I was mistaken, and will waste no more of your time."

"But surely this is the man you knew," Scott said.

"No," I said, fighting tears. "I'm afraid not."

Then I scooped up my coat, made sure the manuscript was tucked safely inside, and crossed to the door. But before my hand reached the knob, Scott was up and had placed the skull on the table and placed a hand upon my arm.

"You were with him when he died," Scott said.

I was silent.

"He must have left you with some vital information," Scott pressed. "Did he have a wife? A lover? Was it you? Who visited him in the hospital? Did he leave children? What were his last words?"

I jerked my arm from beneath his hand.

"I assure you, Mr. Scott," I said, "that even if it requires extraordinary diligence for the rest of my life, I will make sure that you and that hateful woman shall never know."

Then Scott's demeanor melted.

"You must think me a ghoul," he said. "But the truth is I am a desperate man. The newspaper is not a lucrative one, the hours are endless, and my only hope of deliverance is an unvarnished account of Quantrill's terrible and remarkable life. Help me, please."

"You have the subject of your book captive," I said. "Ask him."

Afterword—2008

My great-grandmother was Mary Culhain.

She died in Louisville in 1912, at the age of seventy-seven, and was buried in a clearly marked grave at St. John's Catholic Cemetery, beneath a statue of the Virgin Mary. Her grave is near the cemetery entrance, which now faces Duncan Street, and is not far from the plot where William Clarke Quantrill was originally buried after dying on June 6, 1865.

I did not know Mary Culhain, of course, but she is so part of our family mythology that I feel as if I did; she continued her social and volunteer work in the decades after the Civil War, and in 1888, as a single woman aged fifty-three, she adopted an orphaned Irish baby. That baby was my grandmother, who married and gave birth to my mother in 1923, who married and in turn gave birth to me in 1968. Passed from mother to daughter in my family was the manuscript bound in the leather cover with the stamped rose, with the final few pages taken from beneath the seat at the prison hospital, and always there was the admonition that it was a *private* memoir and not to be shared.

And, just as my great-grandmother did, each generation has collected newspaper clippings and magazine articles that added to the Quantrill story that, if you'll excuse the pun, just refused to die.

William Water Scott, of course, tried to sell the skull.

Less than a week after returning to Dover with it, he wrote the Kansas State Historical Society, urged that the letter be kept secret, and asked, "What would his skull be worth to your society?" The society offered some twenty-five to thirty dollars, but Scott declined, at least temporarily; the mother would soon be dead, he wrote, and beyond any hurt any publicity the newspapers could dish out.

Scott continued to collect material for his book on Quantrill, but travel was difficult because Scott was perpetually broke; sometimes he gave newspaper interviews in which he described his childhood pal as a burgeoning fiend that enjoyed torturing animals. In 1888, he carried the skull from Dover to the historical society at Topeka, and while he did not part with the skull, he did hand over a couple of shinbones. Whether the historical society paid anything for the leg bones is unknown; if it did, the records have since been lost.

In 1889, in a private ceremony, some of the bones taken from the Louisville grave were finally buried in (yet another) unmarked grave in the Dover Fourth Street Cemetery. But Scott kept the skull, at least three arm bones, and a quantity of the faded yellow hair, some of which he sometimes gave as gifts.

Scott died in 1902 of a heart attack, having never written the planned Quantrill biography. Scott's widow sold all of his notes—and the three arm bones—to William Elsey Connelly, secretary of the Kansas historical society. It was a private purchase, however, and Connelly attempted to swap the remains for a number of items he desired more, including a gun purportedly owned by Jesse

James and, in another deal that fell through, a revolver and holster once owned by Wild Bill Hickok.

But in the end, Connelly donated the bones and hair to the society.

Connelly also broke up the many boxes of files that Scott had gathered and sold them to private collectors. After Caroline Cornelia Clarke Quantrill died at the age of eighty-three, the Kansas society announced it would put the bones and hair of Quantrill on public display. Critics suggested they be thrown into the Kaw River instead. The society persisted, however—and pointed out that the bones of John Wilkes Booth were on display in a museum at Washington and that "somewhere" the government had the skeleton of Charles Guiteau, who had murdered James Garfield.

In 1903, the five bones—two shinbones and three arm bones—as well as a vial of his hair, were displayed at the Kansas State Historical Society in a glass case. Lest visitors forget, also in the case was a charred New Testament and a chipped cup from the Lawrence raid.

Although Connelly had broken up Scott's notes, he saved or copied much and used it in part to write *Quantrill and the Border Wars*, published in 1910. For decades, it was considered the definitive biography of the guerrilla chieftain.

The book was popular reading for generations of Kansas schoolchildren, and if you're curious, the book can still be found in many Kansas libraries. Nearly a century old now, it is also in the public domain, and is available on the Internet as a free PDF download from Google.

The book was undoubtedly responsible for demonizing Quantrill to successive generations, because Connelly repeats Scott's assertion that Quantrill displayed a proclivity for evil early in life, and makes little effort to conceal his (understandable) Yankee bias against his subject. But, in at least some sense, W. W. Scott posthumously succeeded in his quest—the best material in Connelly's book is the footnotes that reproduce Scott's notes, and the account of the Louisville exhumation is refreshingly complete for nineteenth-century journalism.

In 1910, the skull of William Clarke Quantrill was passed from W. W. Scott's son, Walter, for use in the initiation rites of the Zeta Chapter of the Alpha Pi fraternity at Dover, Ohio. The skull was shellacked and nicknamed "Jake," but some of the boys knew its real identity from Walter Scott.

According to an account published in a 1981 issue of *Old West* magazine, and authored by a former member of the fraternity, the skull was electrified so that red lights blazed in the eye sockets during the ceremony. Initiates were instructed to place their right hand on the skull and swear loyalty and secrecy to the fraternity. The chapter disbanded in 1942, suffering a crippling decline in membership because of World War II, ending thirty-two years of service for the grinning and red-eyed skull named "Jake"—which, in macabre irony, is longer than Quantrill himself had used the skull in life.

The skull went home with a fraternity trustee and was stored in a basement until 1960, when it was displayed at the fraternity's fiftieth anniversary gathering. In 1972, the skull was given to the Dover Historical Society. A wax head was made, in an attempt to determine a likeness of the living Quantrill, and the skull was placed in a display case. When it wasn't being festooned with red and green ribbons during the historical society's Christmas parties, the head was kept in the museum's refrigerator to keep it from melting, where it impassively watched over the sack lunches of the employees.

Then a shift occurred in cultural attitudes toward the display of human remains in the late 1990s. It seemed improper at best and sacrilegious at worst. A federal law required that all Native American remains be repatriated. The Kansas Legislature followed suit by passing the Unmarked Burial Sites Preservation Act, which provided for a board to oversee the elimination of many hundreds of skeletal remains in the state historical society's collection.

This included the partial remains of Quantrill.

On Saturday morning, October 24, 1992, the bones that W. W. Scott had removed from St. Mary's Catholic Cemetery at Louisville were buried in the old Confederate Memorial Cemetery at Higginsville, in Lafayette County, Missouri.

The bones were carried in a cardboard box to the cemetery by Randy Theis, an archaeologist at the historical museum who was charged with the care of the remains. The night before, Theis had placed the box in his daughter's bedroom for the night, planning to tease her once she is grown that she spent the night with a famous Confederate guerrilla.

Earlier, Theis had separated from the Quantrill bones a left tibia and fibula—the lower leg bones—from an individual of unknown gender who was between seventeen and nineteen years old. The bones were of "unknown provenance," in collections jargon, and at some point had been given the same accession number as the real Quantrill bones—which caused "quite a bit of confusion," as Theis recalled later.

Along with the five bones judged to authentically be Quantrill's, there was a vial of his hair, and these were placed in the grass—the first time the guerrilla chieftain had touched Missouri soil in 127 years. Then the hair and bones were placed in a red plastic Igloo cooler and wedged inside a full-sized coffin made of one-inch oak slabs and historically correct square nails. Also inside the cooler was a sheet of archival acid-free paper that gave a summary of Quantrill's life; then the cooler was epoxied shut and the coffin lid was hammered on with the square nails.

The coffin was draped with a Confederate flag and placed in a church that had once served the old Confederate veteran's home adjacent to the cemetery, under the watchful eyes of an honor guard of Confederate reenactors from the Fifth Missouri Infantry. A Roman Catholic priest read from chapter 5 of John, which tells of Christ's healing at the pool and promises that anyone who believes in Him will not be judged but pass from death to everlasting life. Then the coffin was lifted on the shoulders of men who were blood descendants of Quantrill's men and carried to the grave.

Among the pallbearers was a young man who claimed to be the great-great-grandson of Quantrill. The history buffs in the crowd smirked, because while more than a dozen families claim to be blood descendants of Quantrill, the historical record gives not a hint that the famous guerrilla sired any children.

On October 30, Quantrill's skull was placed in a child's white fiberglass coffin and was buried in the family plot in the Canal Dover Fourth Street Cemetery. Another Catholic priest led the two dozen or so mourners in "Amazing Grace," read the funeral liturgy, and sprinkled the casket with holy water from a plastic squeeze bottle. Then the small casket was buried three feet beneath the surface; the grave diggers were afraid to go deeper for fear of disturbing remains from the 1889 burial.

The inscription on the granite marker reads:

WILLIAM CLARKE QUANTRILL
CAPT MO CAV
CONFEDERATE STATES ARMY
JUL 31 1837   JUN 6 1865

Now there is just one thing left to tell.

At the 1992 burial at Higginsville, after the priest read the burial liturgy and as the reenactors fired twenty-one-gun salutes, an anonymous young woman in period dress came forward and placed a folded black cloth on the lid of the oak coffin. It was unplanned and, most people thought, a bit of drama that was, unfortunately, historically inaccurate; in spite of a famous illustration in *Leslie's Illustrated Weekly*, Quantrill had not literally ridden beneath a black flag emblazoned with his (misspelled) name.

The bundle was not a flag.

I know, because I was the young woman who rushed forward and placed the black cloth on the coffin. I was twenty-four in 1992, and a graduate student in history at the University of Kansas; I was not studying Quantrill, and my thesis was a history of Nicodemus, an all-black town settled by former slaves. I was sick of Quantrill and my great-grandmother's weird manuscript.

I decided the tale should be buried with the purported author, or at least part of him, and perhaps that would release the women of my family from a peculiar burden we had borne for more than a century. Besides having doubts about the truth of the story, I was also sick of having it around. The last thing I needed, while trying to build a career on researching the culture of former slaves, was to have to explain my family's peculiar connection to the most famous of all Confederate guerrillas.

So, as the coffin was being lowered into the ground and I bolted forth and placed the black-wrapped manuscript on the lid, no attempt was made to examine it. I answered no questions about my actions, and stayed just long enough to watch as several hundred pounds of cement was dumped over the casket to discourage grave robbers.

Somewhere of old his ancestors ate the sour grapes which set his teeth on edge. In him was exemplified the terrible and immutable law of heredity. He grew into the gory monster whose baleful shadow falls upon all who share the kindred blood. He made his name a Cain's mark and a curse to those condemned to bear it. The blight of it must fall upon remote generations, those yet unborn and innocent, so inexorable are the decrees of fate and nature. Because of him widows wailed, orphans cried, maidens wept, as they lifted the lifeless forms of loved ones from bloody fields and bore them reeking to untimely graves.

—William Elsey Connelly, *Quantrill and the Border Wars* (1910)

Is there any reward offered either by any individual or state, for the man who killed Quantrill? Who is W. W. Scott? And what does he want with this knowledge? When will his proposed book be out? And will he do justice to me?

—John Langford, the man who claimed to have fired the fatal shot at Wakefield Farm, in a letter to W. W. Scott (1888)

SIGNET

Available From
MAX McCOY

A BREED APART:
A Novel of Wild Bill Hickok

History remembers him as Wild Bill,
but he was born James Butler Hickok,
a young man who forged his future
as a scout on the plains, and as a
Union Spy during the Civil War. But it
was on one afternoon in Springfield,
Missouri, that Hickok found his true
calling—with a revolver in his hand.

SIGNET

Available From
Charles G. West

DUEL AT LOW HAWK

Boot Stoner spent twelve years behind
bars for stealing. Upon his release, he
added murder and kidnapping to his
list—and U.S. Deputy Marshal John
Ward is the only one who stands a
chance of stopping Stoner's
bloody rampage.

"A writer in the tradition of Louis L'Amour and Zane Grey!"
—*Huntsville Times*

National Bestselling Author
RALPH COMPTON

NOWHERE, TEXAS
TRAIN TO DURANGO
DEVIL'S CANYON
AUTUMN OF THE GUN
THE KILLING SEASON
THE DAWN OF FURY
DEATH ALONG THE CIMMARON
RIDERS OF JUDGMENT
BULLET CREEK
FOR THE BRAND
GUNS OF THE CANYONLANDS
BY THE HORNS
THE TENDERFOOT TRAIL
RIO LARGO
DEADWOOD GULCH
A WOLF IN THE FOLD
TRAIL TO COTTONWOOD FALLS
BLUFF CITY
THE BLOODY TRAIL
WEST OF THE LAW
BLOOD DUEL
SHADOW OF THE GUN
DEATH OF A BAD MAN

Available wherever books are sold or at penguin.com

No other series packs this much heat!

THE TRAILSMAN